Highland Destiny

A Guardians of Scotland Novella

By: Victoria Zak

Copyright

Highland Destiny, A Guardians of Scotland Novella

Victoria Zak

Copyright © Victoria Zak, 2015

Edited by: Kathryn Lynn Davis

Cover by: JAB Designs

ISBN-13:

978-1-942516-15-6

Contents

Author Notes

I would like to thank the following people, for without them my dragon lovin' world would not be possible.

To Mr. Zak, my hero, thank you for your support not only in my writing career, but for conquering the hard times with me. I love you!

To my kiddos, my life, thank you for understanding when Mommy has a deadline to meet. I love you!

To my mom and mother-in-law, thank you for your support. We all enjoy Camp Grandma's house. :)

To D.L. Roan, my best friend and writing partner in crime, I adore you! Thank you for being there when I need a shoulder to cry on.

To Zak's Clan, my street team, you all rock my dragon lovin' world!

Chapter One

"Run deep into the Great Glen, child," the auld woman had warned, "where he can no' follow." The crackle in the woman's voice startled Kenna Mackenzie, soon to be Mackintosh, still to this day. It had been over a fortnight since she had been caught off guard by the crone as she made her way through the throng of townsfolk at the marketplace in town. The mysterious, wrinkled, hunchbacked woman approached her, chatting in a tone barely audible. Kenna rubbed her arm, remembering the heated prickle of the woman's touch.

"Yer destiny calls to ye through the flames," the crone intoned.

Before Kenna could question the woman, a man bumped into them, causing a commotion, and the auld woman lost her grip on Kenna's arm. Once settled, the man proclaimed himself clumsy, then pardoned himself. When Kenna turned around to find the woman, she was gone as if she never existed. Kenna furrowed her brows. "Who are ye?" she whispered.

Now, recalling that memory sent a shiver streaking down her spine as she stood by a window in her bedchamber, looking down on the day's festivities.

Straight out of a dream, the morning sun gleamed and chased away any signs of gloomy weather. Chirping birds from a nearby tree teased Mr. Brayly, the keeper of the Mackintosh stronghold, as he tried with all his might to shoo the pests away from above the tables that were set up for their guests. A few hundred clan members were to gather here to witness the Laird of Glenloch, Ian Mackintosh, make his unwavering confession of love to her.

"Kenna Mackintosh," she proclaimed out loud with a sigh. The thought of marrying Ian made her smile and giggle. Today was the happiest day of her life and nothing was going to spoil it, not even haunting words from an auld hag.

At the young age of ten she'd been sent to serve Clan Mackintosh after her parents died during a clan war. William Mackenzie, her uncle, thought it to her benefit to serve the Lady of Glenloch Castle, Ian's mother, to tame the girl's wild side and become a respected lady. As Kenna grew up William often accused his brother of using a light hand when it came to disciplining his daughter. Not that she was a bad child—William believed her to be high-spirited and that she needed to be controlled in order to find a proper husband. Building an alliance with the Mackintoshes would be most beneficial for their clan. Still her spirit was irrepressible.

Fortunately for her uncle, her bloodline was pure. Unfortunately for Kenna, both parents were killed during a clan war when she was young, leaving her in her uncle's custody. Her mother fought hard, like a Mackenzie, beside her husband. Kenna could remember the times when her parents would argue about her mother being on the battlefield. "Woman, ye'll ruin me reputation as a man," her father would warn her. "Behind every good man is a good woman," her mother would reply and bat her eyelashes. Her poor father couldn't resist, so she got her wish.

Throughout her eight years at Glenloch, Kenna proved herself a lady and grew into a beautiful and intelligent lass, gaining the attention of Laird Mackintosh's son, Ian. After the laird's passing, Ian courted her for three years until she turned eight-and-ten and he took over as Laird of Glenloch and Clan Chief of the Mackintoshes.

Though Kenna knew her uncle's true motives were to marry her into a powerful clan for his own profit, she thought herself blessed to find Ian charming and extremely handsome. There was something about the way his sandy blond hair hung freely just past his ear lobes that made her go weak in the knees. And his eyes… she had never seen a more alluring golden yellow so vibrant.

Most lassies couldn't say the same regarding their betrothed. In fact they were envious. In true Mackintosh fashion, Ian exemplified dominance and chivalrous charm without saying a word, and he continued the clan's good name. His people loved and honored him as they had his father. Still, Kenna felt uncomfortable at social gatherings as if she didn't belong. Even though time had passed since her days as Ian's mother's servant, she was still considered unworthy in the eyes of the clan. Whether it be a swooning lass or kinsmen wanting to discuss clan business, all eyes were on Ian Mackintosh.

Kenna hung her head and stared at the ground as she thought about standing next to Ian at the ceremony. Judgmental eyes would be fixed on her. She could hear the hisses and whispers now. *How could the laird marry a servant lass?*

Exhaling heavily, Kenna lifted her chin and focused on the present. In time the voices would quiet down, and again she would prove she was worthy of Ian and deserved to be a member of Clan Mackintosh.

A knock on her bedchamber door startled her. "My lady," a woman's voice called, "are ye ready for me to prepare yer hair?"

Her hair? Kenna panicked. Had she mused the morn away? With haste, she went to her bed where her handmaiden had laid out her wedding dress while Kenna bathed earlier. Ian had chosen the fabric and given it to her as a betrothal gift. Time had slipped by; she hadn't dressed and was still wearing her shift. "I'm terribly sorry, Sarah. I'm a wee bit behind." Kenna pulled the ruby-red dress over her head then slipped her arms through the long, wide sleeves. "I'll be only a minute."

Sarah huffed, "Ye'll be late to yer own funeral, lass."

Kenna wiggled her shoulders, trying to straighten the dress over her body. "Aye, Sarah, ye be right." Kenna smiled, knowing she had teased and gotten under Sarah's skin. Sarah was quite a bit older than Kenna, a no nonsense woman.

"I'll be back soon and ye'd better be ready for me." Kenna could hear Sarah's heavy footsteps as she marched down the corridor.

Sighing in relief, Kenna laced up the front of her dress. As she bent down to slip on her shoes the room spun and her vision doubled. She shut her eyes. "Nay, this can no' be happening again." Trepidation crashed over her as a vision of a child flashed before her.

As a wee bairn, and afterwards, Kenna had had visions. Visions she couldn't explain and did not wish to see. They came to her in flashes, unexpectedly random, and warned her of things to come. But since her parents' death the premonitions had stopped. Or so she thought.

She gripped her head to try and stop the throbbing, though she knew from the past that the pain wouldn't go away until she opened her eyes and allowed herself to see the portent. Kenna felt her way around the room, knocking over a candelabra along the way. Finally she reached her dressing table and braced herself for what was to come. She opened her eyes and stared into the mirror.

Brown eyes as big as chestnuts blinked back at her as she attempted to clear the double vision. The room swayed and the mirror took on a form of its own. Small circular ripples appeared in the middle of the oval glass, spreading into bigger waves. It was as if she were looking through water after a stone had been thrown into it. The mirror took on depth like a tunnel, at the end of which lay her vision.

She saw a woman wearing her red wedding dress, dancing with Ian. They were happy, in love. The passion between them was so intense she could feel it from where she stood. Without seeing a face she couldn't tell who the bride was. Then another flash, another vision. The woman was looking down at her swollen belly. She was with child. Then Ian walked into the room and the mother lifted her head to greet him as she rubbed her belly.

Kenna gasped. It was her. She braced her hands on the table as she felt her knees begin to buckle.

The mirror rippled farther, deeper than before. Another flash hit Kenna hard; she doubled over, clenching her stomach as it knotted and felt tight. *What is happening to me?*

She couldn't tear herself away from the vision, for this time she saw herself in bed with sweat beading on her forehead and her hair stuck to her face and neck. A determined midwife pushed her up into a sitting position and told her to push. The pain-struck scream ripped through her body, then there was an eerie silence.

Kenna's pains were gone, but not the fear or tension in the room.

Kenna straightened when she heard a cry from a newly born babe. "A babe?" She blinked back the tears that were collecting in her eyes so she could see what lay in front of her. There was a sense of calm rushing over her as she squinted deeper into the mirror.

"Tis a boy!" The midwife beamed as she handed the babe to Kenna. The labor had been long and hard, leaving her exhausted, but somehow she found the strength to hold her son. She looked down at the crying babe and smiled. He was exactly like his father already, demanding and gathering an audience as Ian and his mother rushed into the bedchamber.

"Och, Kenna, ye be a bonny mum." Ian hurried over to her bedside to catch the first glimpse of his son. He looked at the babe, then back to Kenna. "A son. I have a son." The gratification in Ian's voice said it all. He was proud to produce a son, which left Kenna beyond the moon and stars happy.

His mother looked over his shoulder while he held the babe. She smiled as she lifted the blanket from the babe's now sleeping body. "Ye did good, me son." She grimly glanced at Kenna as she covered the babe back up. Kenna felt a cold chill race down her spine as she held Lady Mackintosh's cold stare. This is odd, she thought as she watched Ian's mother leave the room. What had she seen?

"Ian, may I?" She held her hands out, reaching for her son.

"Aye, my love." Placing the sleeping bundle in her arms, he bent down and kissed her forehead. "Our wee laddie will rule the world one day."

Kenna returned his smile. Ian was definitely overjoyed, which made Kenna feel happy that she had pleased her husband. Her world was complete and she couldn't wait to give him more sons.

"I'll leave ye be to rest." Ian kissed his wife then turned and headed for the door.

Once alone, Kenna was more and more curious about Lady Mackintosh's odd behavior. Even Ian was acting a little peculiar. Never before had she seen him so pleased.

It was probably the exhaustion taking over, yet she couldn't shake that icy stare that had chilled her to the core. Not wasting another minute, Kenna laid her son on her lap and slowly unfolded the blanket. She held his tiny hand in hers and counted his fingers; five on both hands. "Tis good." Then she uncovered more of the babe, reaching his toes. And they too were as perfect as they could be. She kissed his feet, which made the babe wiggle. Kenna giggled. The babe looked up at her and blinked his eyes. They were full and golden, like Ian's. Odd, she thought, as she looked deep into his eyes. The yellow irises swirled around a slit pupil. Kenna shut her eyes, not believing what she saw. She had to be tired.

Hesitantly, she opened her eyes one at a time, relieved that her son's eyes were normal again.

Kenna backed away from the dressing table and shook her head. This had to be her nerves playing devilish tricks on her. But surely having visions did not make her a beast? Fed up with the trickery, she turned to walk away when another flash rippled the glass. Her blood turned to ice. She swore she was not going to look into that mirror—not when her body was shaking terribly with fear of what was to come. There was danger lurking behind her—she could feel it in the pit of her stomach. But what if the vision was a warning? Perhaps Ian was in danger or worse, her unborn son. If it meant she could steer her future, she had to turn around.

She slowly glanced over her shoulder, praying there was nothing there to fear, but she knew better than to cling to false hope. In order to move past the throbbing in her head, she turned around and stared into the mirror. Horror unlike anything she had ever felt before crashed against her. She gasped, her eyes widened, and her heart thumped against her ribcage, her body heated from the flames that licked through her vision. She wrenched back from the scene and her hands flew over her mouth, holding back a scream that threatened to escape at any moment. Even though the sight froze her, it was the overwhelming feeling of darkness that consumed her. The babe's eyes were no longer kind and playful; they were haunted and dark. His soul was no longer honorable, it was full of greed. He was a tyrant to his people.

Kenna had to look away. How could this be? Her son, her handsome son would grow up to be an evil man. She shook her head, trying to erase the gruesome image. Perhaps she had turned away too soon. Perhaps there was more to her vision. Kenna faced the mirror of doom one last time. Wings? There were wings. Kenna stepped back until she hit the bed with the back of her knees.

The vision faded into the flow of ripples and disappeared, returning the mirror back to normal. The space was calm like nothing had ever happened; however it had. Kenna's happily ever after came crashing to the floor. The darkness she felt had eaten away at her, leaving her empty inside. A demon? She thought. How could this be? Her son a demon?

What was she going to do? She paced the floor in deep thought. How was she going to tell her husband-to-be what she'd seen? She wasn't. It wasn't as though she could explain to Ian that she had visions or tell him their son would become a demon, when she could not explain *how* she knew herself. Her visions were never wrong. And she knew how the vision made her feel—pure evil. Certainly Ian would think she had gone mad or, worse, condemn her of witchery. And everyone knew the fate of unholy, spell-casting hags. She was not about to end up dangling from a tree, nor wind up the townsfolk's kindling. *Burn the witch, burn the witch!* She could hear them chant. Nay, she had to keep her secrets... alone.

Kenna's heart sank farther into the darkness as she thought about preventing her vision from coming true. There was only one way to prevent it. *She could not marry Ian.*

For several moments she was frozen by the magnitude of the thought. Her whole life, her love, her family—gone in an instant. But the will her uncle had never succeeded in suppressing came rushing back in all its power and determination. *I have to be strong. Stronger than*

11

I've ever been before. She had to go before her charming Ian changed her mind. Before she changed her own mind. She held fast to the evil she had seen and felt, letting it force her forward.

She strode to the window, looking for a way to escape without being caught. But how, when there were people milling around outside the ceremony area and the castle was alive with maids bustling down corridors? And forget about sneaking out through the kitchen, which was undoubtedly the center of all the chaos today. What was she going to do?

If she were caught, Ian would be livid with her for causing such a scene—and embarrassing him by trying to run away. Furthermore, she would be forced to tell the truth. Sarah would be returning soon. She had to come up with a plan...fast. Kenna paced a small area in front of the window, thinking of ways to get away. As she was about to give up hope, a thought came to her. *If everyone is preoccupied with wedding preparations, then maybe I could slip past the chaos unnoticed.* Kenna paused and thought out the rest of her plan. *Run deep into the Great Glen, child, where he can no' follow.* The auld woman's warning haunted her again. Everything from the very fiber of her being to the pit of her core told her to do as the crone had said. To run and somehow find the Great Glen. She couldn't explain the desperate need to go, but she believed her future depended on it.

With haste, Kenna took her black cloak from her trunk and swung it over her shoulders. She lifted the hood and made sure her hair was tucked in so no one would recognize her, then quit the bedchamber. Keeping her head down, with quickened strides and a wee bit of luck, she dodged a few maids and guardsmen on her way to the kitchen. In no time, Kenna blended into the hustle and bustle. Once she made it out the back door, she closed it tight, rested her back against the big wooden door and closed her eyes, for she had to calm her nerves and keep her chest from bursting from the fear of being sought out. Her body tensed in anticipation of leaving Glenloch. She exhaled. *Breathe, Kenna breathe.*

When she opened her eyes, she spotted the tree line of the glen beyond the nearest hill. She looked to the right and then to the left. No one was around and she had a clear shot into the woods. Kenna pushed off the door, took in a deep breath, and with god speed she raced toward the forest.

She ran deeper and deeper into the thick glen, tears streaming down her face as she considered everything she was leaving behind. She didn't dare look behind her for one last glance at Glenloch, aware that if she did she would turn and find her way back to the fairytale life that once had been hers. Nay, she had to leave and embark on her new life, far away from Ian. She had to save her unborn son.

Kenna stopped dead in her tracks when a thatch-roofed cottage came into view. Smoke billowed from its roof and the door was open, inviting her in. Could this be what the auld woman warned her about? Kenna hid behind a nearby tree, watching the cottage for any sign of movement. There was none, only a peaceful cottage in the woods, as if it had been here waiting for her all along.

Once Kenna was convinced she was alone, she crept up the stone steps and into the cottage. A sense of calm replaced all fear as she looked around the small, cozy area. Everything she could ever want was here. A hearth, big enough to hang a black cauldron from an iron spit, consumed most of one wall. In the middle of the room a table sat with all sorts of knives and files for wood working arranged upon it. A small bed from across the room called to her exhausted body.

Unable to stand any longer, she plopped down on the bed and curled into a ball. She had never felt so alone. The quietness of the cottage was too loud. Kenna pressed her hands over her ears to block out the sound as images of the day collided inside her, and before long she cried herself to sleep with Ian on her mind.

Chapter Two

Five years later

1315

A massive shadowy winged reflection danced over the clear blue loch as Dragonkine warrior Rory Cameron flew over the Great Glen. As if the water had been beckoning him, he swooped down to land. The ground thundered, the trees shook, and a ripple undulated across the loch as he landed hard near the water's edge. A gush of air swept through the sand as Rory snorted in frustration. He shook his head and folded his wings as he settled and readied himself for the transition.

Now in human form, the Highlander's mood went from foul to worse. He'd assumed a good long fly through the glen would ease his troubled mind, but he had been terribly mistaken. Since he was Dragonkine and could shift into a powerful dragon, he should be able to find a way to overcome his urges. But not Rory.

Lying with nameless women soothed his dragon's needs, for his dragon was one overly masculine beast, relentless when it came to bedding a lass. Not even Rory's prized stallion had the vigor to compete with his dragon's vitality. Fortunately for Rory, he possessed a gallant and

15

charming personality that the lassies found irresistible. Unfortunately for the lass in his sights for the night, or mayhap two, he wasn't one who stayed until morn. It had never been a problem for Rory as long as he stuck to his rules. Once he focused on his prey, he was blunt about the stakes. First, no commitment. Second, leave your heart in your pocket. There was to be no love, only a night filled with lust and hot dirty sex. And for Rory, the dirtier the better. And third, he promised to always leave the lass blissfully fulfilled.

As of late, his lifestyle left him unsatisfied no matter how good the bedding was, whether it be with one lass or two. Something was missing. He had an itch that couldn't be scratched.

He bent down and picked up a flat rounded rock, tossing it up in the air and catching it a few times as he mused. What he couldn't figure out was what had changed. Aye, his fellow Dragonkine kin were up against King Drest, their dragon king, and his determination to wreak revenge against humans. Thus far, Rory could care naught about their war and what would happen to Scotland. All he could think about was how lucky his commander, James the Black Douglas and his wife Abigale were to have such an undying love between them. Conall and his wife Effie had found love through a storm of troubles. Every Dragonkine warrior had a mate to soothe his dragon side, to make him whole.

With a flick of his wrist Rory sent the rock skipping across the water's surface, letting out his frustrations. As he stood watching the ripples disappear back into the placid waters, he thought he saw a reflection wavering there. In it, he stood bending his head down to a woman cradled gently at his side. A ripple of loneliness went through him. Everyone else had a mate. Where was his? He was stunned to realize what was making him feel like a ball of tightly spun wool. He needed to find his mate.

Shaking his head, he expunged the thought, for finding a mate went against all his rules. He would have to commit, and he swore that wasn't going to happen; although his soul told him differently. Rory ran a hand down his face, exhaled, then looked up to the blue sky, frustrated and confused. A mate? A female to devote his life to? Love? Surely not. But how was he going to find her and gain her acceptance for who he truly was? Alas, his past had been unsavory when it came to females. His thoughts were a jumble of impulses he did not know how to control.

Besides, he had to admit he was becoming fonder of the idea of finding a lass his soul could connect with. His cock twitched thinking about this unknown lass. To be able to look into his mate's eyes and see his reflection—a complete man. To be able to dance in the flames of passion. To be loved unconditionally. That was exactly what he was missing. He cared naught what the lass looked like as long she made him feel alive.

But where was he going to find such a rare lass? She sure as hell wasn't back home within Black Stone on the Hill. He'd conquered every female within sight of the castle walls and come up with his ballocks in a knot. He expected that his exceptional tracking abilities would lead him on his search, but he had come up empty handed. Besides, Dragonkine warriors could sense their mates from a great distance, so what was wrong with him? Indeed, he could go from village to village to seek her, but that would take time, and time wasn't on his side. He was one of the Seven Guardians and he had a job to do; to protect Scotland and her people. His commander, James, needed him back at Black Stone with his decision. Would he stay with the Brotherhood or join King Drest?

It wasn't too long ago that the Kine had found out that Drest had been awakened and lingered underground, waiting to rise again. If he rose, he would seek out his revenge on every human for the treason that had been brought upon Dragonkine centuries ago. MacAlpin, King of Scots, had tricked Drest, inviting him and his seven royals to a gathering to unite the two kingdoms. Little did the dragons know that MacAlpin had no intentions of working together with the Kine. As the tension in the great hall succumbed to ale-drunken men, the human king opened trapdoors, sending King Drest and his men to their deaths, impaled by spikes.

And if MacAlpin's treason wasn't bad enough, the aftermath of his actions only worsened when he led an all-out war on the Kine and their females. The dragon elders intervened before the human king completely destroyed Dragonkine. A compromise was made; MacAlpin would cease the war and allow only seven Dragonkine warriors to live and serve a long line of human kings. The rest of the dragons and their females had to be destroyed.

With the dragons almost defeated, the elders had no choice but to agree.

It wasn't a matter of if Drest would rise again, it was a matter of when. Seeing his family suffer at the hands of humans, Rory believed that the Dragonkine needed their own king and it sickened him to bow down to a human. However, his bloodline was one of the purest of the Guardians. Generations of his lineage had made the sacred vow, to protect the humans. In order to survive, Rory had to make the same oath.

Now, with James and his second-in-command married to humans, the idea of a dragon king rule was unsavory. Rory respected his brethren and didn't want to turn his back on them, but he couldn't resist the idea of having a dragon, his kind, as king. Time was running out and Rory had to choose sides, but not today.

Rory gazed toward the horizon. *Smoke?* With his heightened eyesight, he could see smoke coming from deep within the glen. His body stiffened as he sniffed the air. Burning earth invaded his senses, but there was more than just smoke. He couldn't place it, nonetheless he was drawn to the scent like a moth to a flame. Rory clenched his jaw, fighting the strong urge that rocked him so hard he felt he might fall over. His dragon wanted out.

With all his efforts to resist failing terribly and his body being taken over by an overbearing dragon, Rory

19

began to shift. In a flash his skin changed from sun kissed tan to green shimmering scales. Starting from the top of the dragon's head, rows of small spikes streaked down his neck and increased in size, stopping at the end of his tail. His nostrils flared as he inhaled more of that intriguing scent. Sharp, curved talons gripped the sandy shoreline as he took off in a full run, one thundering stride after another until he gained enough speed to take to the sky. With a flap of his massive wings, he was airborne and headed straight for the billowing smoke.

Once he drew near, he glided right and swooped down closer to the ground. "God's teeth!" Rory was shocked as a wall of flames came into view as high as the tallest tree in the forest framing a small cottage. *What could have had happened to cause the fire?* Lightning? Nay. Rain had been scarce for at least a fortnight. Perhaps he had flown upon an innocent forest fire.

Odd, the flames aren't spreading; they're staying in one place. Since his commander was a fire-breathing dragon, Rory had seen his fair share of destructive flames. With this magnitude, the fire should have already engulfed the cottage.

Rory hovered above the flames as he searched for a way to douse the fire. He dodged a blaze reaching for his stomach. "Shite!" Then it hit him like a bolt of lightning. It was that intoxicating scent again. It had lured him here, awakening all his dragon senses. He circled the cottage from above, trying to follow the essence. It was absolutely driving him daft. It had to be coming from inside the cottage.

His spikes vibrate as he felt eyes rake over him. Out of pure instinct a low growl escaped his throat. The perfume was so inebriating he couldn't think straight. All he could focus on was that honeysuckle scent...or was it the beautiful woman staring at him through the window of the cottage?

Chapter Three

It had been five years to the day since Kenna Mackenzie set foot in this cottage and withdrew from the outside world. Her new life was very difficult at first. At night she found herself frightened of all the unseen and the unexplained noises coming from the glen. On her own for the first time, she found ways to protect herself from those unknown threats, even if she had to stack furniture in front of the door and set traps for any unexpected guests.

After the noises became identifiable, the loneliness set in. That was until one day while on a hunt she found a wounded wolf pup hiding underneath a thicket of blackthorn. The pup snarled and snapped at her when she bent down to examine its wounds. Despite the wolf's protests she picked the critter up and noticed that his back right leg was badly lacerated. Kenna couldn't leave the poor thing out in the glen to fend for itself or be eaten by a beastie. She took it home, nursed his wounds and over time they bonded and learned to trust one another. Not so small anymore, the pup had grown into a huge gray wolf and now lay at Kenna's feet as she sat at the table tinkering with her latest invention.

The wolf lifted his head and growled. "Finn? What is it, lad?" Kenna dropped her file when Finn stalked toward the door. She had been filing and shaping a piece of wood for hours, hoping it would turn into the weapon she envisioned. Since she'd neglected him most of the day, she supposed Finn wanted her attention. "Och, Finn." She walked over to the wolf, who was vigorously scratching at the front door. "What's gotten into ye?" She reached down to calm him, but he backed away and looked up at her impatiently, wanting to go outside. Kenna opened the door and he bolted.

Kenna peeked out and saw nothing alarming. She shook her head and walked back inside, leaving the front door cracked in case Finn decided to return. The wolf was more to her than an animal—she considered him a friend. Whether she hunted or picked herbs, they were inseparable.

One day on the way home from hunting, Kenna and Finn met a gypsy woman. At first Kenna didn't trust the woman. For all that she knew the woman might be one of Ian's spies. Over time the auld woman proved herself trustworthy, and now Kenna and the wolf looked forward to her company.

The woman would bring them food and any supplies they needed. Not that Kenna needed much. She was self-sufficient. She made her own clothes, harvested her own food when the climate was giving, and she made her own weapons. If she needed something, she worked with the gypsy and traded her weapons for supplies. Regardless of what she needed, Kenna enjoyed the auld woman's company.

Kenna sat back down, brushing off Finn's odd behavior and picked up her file. The wolf had probably sensed the auld woman coming for a visit, she thought. Kenna paused, her brows furrowed. It wasn't time for the gypsy to return. Then she felt the heat—the flames were back. "Damn dragon," she whispered under her breath as she marched over to the window. She pushed the fur aside and searched the glen for a sign the dragon had returned. He'd come back to torch her home, she knew it. Although she hadn't seen evidence of that, it had to be a dragon. What else was big enough to conjure flames as high as the sky? No mortal man had the ability to create a blaze as massive as the one that kept her caged within her land. Every time she had the courage to venture past the row of old yew trees, a wall of flames would appear, preventing her from passing. The dragon was toying with her as if she was some kind of plaything.

Seclusion had its advantages and also its shortcomings. If Kenna ever spoke a word about the odd coincidences she had witnessed here many times, they would lock her up in the dungeons. Aye, she believed in the things that go bump in the night and loomed in the shadows of the glen. But if she had to pick the most interesting creatures she had met, it would have to be the Fae. She had felt their light and experienced their trickery a time or two. Arriving back home from hunting only to find her furniture turned upside down or to find her herb shelf reorganized tended to get a wee bit frustrating. So

24

for her to say that dragons didn't exist would be odd in itself.

This time she would be ready for the beastie.

Kenna truly thought she mayhap be going daft, for there was no sign of the dragon except for the fire, she glimpsed a winged beast hovering above the flames, flapping its wings as if it was taunting her. Her heart sped up and her eyes widened in astonishment. The bloody thing was more massive than any creature she had ever seen. Its wings were twice the size of her house and the spikes perched on its back looked lethal. "Shite." Kenna stepped in front of the window, trying to follow the dragon with her eyes, but it had flown out of her sight.

Fed up with this cat and mouse game, Kenna grabbed one of her inventions; the one she called Dragon Slayer. She purposely made it to do just that. The impressive weapon consisted of a masterfully carved oaken stock with a forged iron bow. She used an ingenious mechanism to prepare the bowstring and razor-sharp bolt, and a trigger to unleash the fury. While it had taken time to master, the armament was incredibly well-balanced and deadly accurate. Perfect for bringing down prey from the sky.

With Dragon Slayer in her sweaty hand, Kenna strode back to the window for one last look. Quickly she yanked the furs away and immediately froze. One huge dark eye peeked in at her and swirled intensely when Kenna came into view. Once she could feel her legs again, she took a step back. "Beastie," she whispered.

The dragon moved slowly, stalking her. The green beast turned its head and sniffed the air as if he was smelling her. Hot breath gusted through the window, blowing her long brown hair as the dragon exhaled.

"I will no' be yer dinner," Kenna seethed through gritted teeth. Staring down the beast, she gripped her weapon and was about to run out the door when she heard Finn howl. "Finn," She gasped. If that dragon hurt Finn…God help her.

Bolting from the cottage, Kenna positioned Dragon Slayer in her arms, ready to use it. She skidded around the side of the cottage right where the dragon had been only seconds before. She came to an abrupt halt when the dragon was nowhere to be seen. "What?" *Where could it have gone?* A howl from Finn brought Kenna's attention to the back of the cottage. "Finn!" she cried out and ran toward the howl.

Panic waned when she reached her wolf. "Thank God!" Kenna ran over to Finn, who stood staring up at the sky, growling. Kenna squinted up to where Finn's gaze was locked. "By the saints!" The green beast was above them, flapping its wings as if he was treading water. Without a second thought, she aimed Dragon Slayer at her target. As she pulled the trigger, a deadly bolt raced toward the dragon, embedding itself in the beast's right wing. A blood-curdling screech echoed throughout the Great Glen. Kenna followed her target with her eyes as it spiraled to the ground. The forest trees shook and the loud thud made Kenna jump.

Stunned, she couldn't believe she'd actually wounded the massive beast. Finn took off like hell fire toward the fallen dragon with Kenna close behind. Where they were headed the forest was thick with vegetation. Staying on guard with her hand on her weapon, Kenna hopped over a fallen tree and continued to follow Finn until he came to a stop in front of a thicket. Was the dragon close? Deep down Kenna really didn't want to find out, however she had to make sure the beast was dead, for if it wasn't, she would have to finish the job or become one of the dragon's many victims.

The eerie silence cut through her and shook her to the core as she gained enough courage to peek through the bushes. She looked down at Finn and met his persistent blue gaze as he nudged her leg with his nose. "Och, Finn, I'm going, I'm going." Kenna crouched down and peeled back a branch full of green leaves and…thorns. "Ouch." Blood was pooling at the tip of her pricked finger. She stuck it in her mouth to stop the bleeding.

As she wriggled through the bushes, she couldn't believe her eyes. A man lay face up, without a stitch of clothing. Finn stalked the body when Kenna called him back. "Nay." She shooed him away as she took two steps forward. Her first thought was that the dragon had claimed another victim, but the bolt sticking out of the man's shoulder told her differently. She froze in disbelief; her heartbeat stilled for a long moment. She had shot the bolt into a dragon, but it was now lodged in a man. *What is happening here?* She glared at Finn as if he might have an answer. Her heart raced and she shuddered. She did not think she would ever move again, but she must.

Gingerly taking the blunt end of Dragon Slayer she nudged the man's outer thigh. "Get up," she called to him. When he didn't respond, her heart sank. "How could this have happened?" Kenna shook her head. Certainly she wasn't daft, there had been a dragon and she'd wounded it, yet here lay a man brought down by her hand.

Curious about this man and going against her better judgment, she kneeled down beside him and dropped her weapon, keeping it close by as she gazed upon his body. She had never seen a man of this stature before. His skin looked as if it had been kissed by the sun. Reluctantly she reached out to place her hand on his broad chest to see if he was still breathing, but then held back. Thinking it better not to touch him, she balled her fist to resist the temptation. *Look but don't touch,* she warned herself. More and more curious, she watched sweat slide off the hard ridges of his muscled abdomen. Her eyes followed those ridges farther down until she blushed and turned away.

After the discomfort faded Kenna felt a strong urge to see his face, hidden under black shoulder-length hair that concealed his identity. With a trembling hand she reached across his body and softly brushed the strands away from his face. She gasped. The man was truly handsome. She pursed her lips as she ran the back of her fingers down his cheek to the stubble of his jawline. This time she allowed herself to go farther down his neck to his chest. That's when she noticed the bolt again, lodged into his shoulder.

Feeling guilty and utterly sorry for wounding him, she had to help. "I'm sorry." Kenna wrinkled her nose and turned her head away as she pulled the bolt from his shoulder. He didn't move, not even a flinch. "Dear God in heaven, what have I done?" Blood poured from the hole as soon as the bolt left it. Kenna tore a strip of cloth from the bottom of her long tunic, unbuckled her belt then turned back to the man. If she didn't act fast he could lose a lot of blood, or worse, his arm.

After a few intense minutes, she had the belt wrapped tight around his upper shoulder and the wound bandaged. With blood on her hands she wiped them on her leather trews and looked the man over one last time. His chest rose and fell, but for how long? She was not about to stay around and find out. She planned to be long gone before he woke and confronted his attacker.

Kenna stood with a heavy heart as she gazed down on his body. Something was nagging at her, telling her not to leave him. She couldn't shake the feeling that she knew him, yet she had never met this man before. Fighting temptation she turned around and started to trek back through the woods to her cottage. Suddenly she realized Finn hadn't followed. "Finn!" She looked behind her and to her astonishment…he was sitting next to the man. "Come on, Finn. We have to leave now."

Finn looked at the man then back at Kenna.

29

"No, no, no, Finn. We leave now." Kenna put her foot down and Finn laid down, unwavering in his determination. "He will be fine. I fixed his wound." The stubborn wolf let out a shrill whine and nipped at the air.

Kenna shrugged her shoulders and irritably slapped her hands on her thighs. "And what do ye expect me to do? Bring him home with us?"

Finn stood and lowered his head as if he was agreeing to her suggestion.

Kenna scowled at her friend. The sweet wee pup she had rescued looked as if he was choosing sides—and it wasn't hers.

"Ye're a traitor, Finn." Kenna huffed back to the man and viewed the area. "How aboot we hide him over there?" Kenna pointed to a hollowed-out yew tree.

Finn growled.

"Fine," Kenna bit back as she bent at the waist and picked up the man's feet and pulled. Hopefully the path back home would be clearer than the one that led them here.

The long hike home, dragging a man's listless body in tow, grew to be a daunting and challenging task, especially when Kenna shimmied the man up the last step and into her cottage. At one point in time she tried to sit the Highlander up as she pushed and heaved on his back to get him up the first step. To her dismay she slipped and landed on her arse in the dirt. She was surprised he hadn't come to after she'd banged his head multiple times throughout the trek, and now she had done it again as she pulled a little too hard and his head bounced off the last step. "Shite. Sorry." Kenna wrinkled her face, knowing it must have hurt.

Once inside, she left the man on the floor, dragged herself over to her bed and grabbed a fur and a blanket. She laid them on the ground, for she had no strength left to try to lift this Highlander up and into her bed. The floor would have to do. First she placed the fur, then rolled the man on top of the billowing layers. She then tucked a blanket around him, making sure he wouldn't catch his death. After she was done she stood exhausted, but he still needed her help. She had to clean the wound and ease his pain; she had a plan.

Quickly she went to her herb shelf, fumbling through the small ceramic jars. "Where are my self-heal leaves? Lemon balm, nay. Blessed thistle, nay, wolfsbane." She picked up the jar, deciding if this ointment would do the trick and ease his pain. "Nay." She put the jar back on the shelf. "It might work for pain, but the hallucinations would be horrible." She searched some more, then stopped, defeated, when she realized that self-heal was missing. "Maiden, mother, crone," she huffed with her hands on her hips. "Bloody Fae." As she expected, the flighty mischievous ones had been at it again, breaking into her cottage and taking things that didn't belong to them, all to give themselves a good chuckle. But this time Kenna wasn't laughing. She desperately needed those leaves to ease the man's pain.

"Finn, come. We need to find some self-heal, and fast." Kenna took one last baffled glance at the wounded man who lay perfectly still, bundled in a thick blanket, before she left in search of the healing herb. She couldn't explain the day's occurrences, as she couldn't explain why she had foresight into her future. There was a dragon; she'd felt him, seen him. And the flames were always there, keeping her secluded and within the boundaries of her land. She shook her head. "Kenna, ye be going daft." Although her mind was a big muddled mess, one thought remained; *I have to help this man and hopefully find forgiveness for my impulsive behavior.*

Shaking free of her thoughts, Kenna crossed the room and headed outside with Finn following close behind. She knew exactly where to find the purple leaves because she had planted them there not too long ago. The small plowed area full of herbs was not far from her cottage, right before the giant bog myrtle. Although nothing soothed her more than tinkering with her weapons, planting and harvesting herbs came close. It had to be the way her hands and fingers warmed as she dug through the earth in the summer, for winters were too wet and brutally cold to be outside in the elements. She collected herbs throughout the warmer months in hopes that she would have enough remedies to aid her through the year. And by the looks of her lush garden, she would be well-stocked for the coming winter.

"There." Kenna briskly strode over to the purple plant, careful not to disturb the meadowsweet. Quickly, she tore off a few leaves that were the perfect size for covering his wound. Kenna had turned to go back to the cottage when she stopped, disbelieving her own eyes. Her heart plummeted and her blood raced with adrenaline. The cottage was engulfed in violent flames. "Flames? How? The dragon is…" As if the devil himself was chasing her, Kenna ran with god speed to her cottage, praying she would make it in time to save the man.

Chapter Four

The door shut heavily and Rory opened one eye, confirming he was alone. A grin spread across his masculine face, enhancing his deep dimples, one on each cheek. His body felt like it was going to burst into a million flickering stars when he recalled how his mate had made him feel alive again. When he was in the sky all he could do was surrender to his dragon's persistent urge to find its mate. He was being reckless when he looked into her window, but he couldn't control himself or his dragon. He had to see her, even if it meant terrifying her in the process.

Though she had struck him as beautiful in his dragon's eyes, nothing compared to feasting his eyes on her as a human. Oh aye, he'd taken his fill of her beauty, basking in that sweet honeysuckle scent while she assaulted his skin with feathery caresses back in the forest. 'Twas only fair. Although it proved a risky game he amused himself with—he was almost caught watching her.

Every time Rory closed his eyes, a sweet, torturing image of Kenna invaded his thoughts. His flesh pricked and ached to feel her again. He recalled the tickle of the tip of her long, brown braid, teasing his skin when she bent over and tended to his wound. He imagined reaching up and thrusting his hands through those silken strands and pulling her down to taste her plump, full lips. His cock still throbbed and it had been hours since their meeting in the glen. "God's bones." Rory sat up and his head spun. The fall had injured him more than the bloody arrow, but he'd had to make the fall look convincing enough for his mate to want to help a poor wounded man, instead of trying to kill a beastly dragon.

Indeed fear had shone through her eyes and he felt every bit of it. A massive, overbearing dragon, overstepping its boundaries would strike terror even in the courageous. Shifting back to a Highlander and approaching her as human would have been the proper thing to do. *Aye, but when have I ever proclaimed to be proper?*

The woolen blanket slipped off, leaving him naked as he stood taking in the cottage's quaint eccentric qualities. Rory meandered through the kitchen. He inspected the area, picking up a wooden bowl, appreciating the craftsmanship as his attention was drawn beyond to a table full of carrots and neeps. Freshly baked bread cooled next to a bundle of mixed herbs; his stomach growled. *'Tis a good sign.* With the way he ate, he needed a mate who could cook.

Continuing his tour to the other side of the cottage, he noticed a wall of weapons he had never seen before. His interest piqued, he walked over to the weapon his mate had used to take down the dragon. A menacing yet beautiful thing. He picked it up, assuming it would be heavy. *Feather-light*. He traced his finger down the taut string in admiration of the quality of workmanship. He smiled. His mate was truly amazing.

But why did she have all these weapons in her possession? She was the only one out here living in the cottage, for he would be able to smell another who was anywhere near, especially if it was male. He smelled only her. Bewildered and alarmed, Rory started to have second thoughts. Mayhap he had been too distracted about finding a mate and walked right into a trap. Ever since the Dragonkine made their presence known, a few egotistical, envious men were rumored to have put a bounty on all dragons, dead or alive. Aye, a massive dragon head hanging on a hunter's wall next to a Highland stag would boost any man's hunting prowess threefold. If they only knew what a dragon was capable of, they would renounce the bounty and look the other way when encountering one.

Although this was a troubled time for Scotland, Dragonkine had had more than their share of hard times. It all started back in the days before Kenneth MacAlpin was crowned king; back in the days when Dragonkine had their own king, King Drest; back in the days when humans and Dragonkine lived together in harmony. All peace had been broken when MacAlpin became greedy and wanted to rule over the Scots *and* Kine. One brutal attack left Rory's Kine forever at the mercy of humans. And they had lost all of their females, which left the remaining Kine without their mates. Without their soul's match a dragon became unpredictable, deadly.

Dragonkine only mated with Dragonkine females, however his two brethren had recently paired with human mates. *Aye, this could be a trap.*

Not knowing how much time he had before the brown-haired lass returned, Rory strode over to the kitchen area and grabbed a sharp knife. If in fact the lass had plans to give away his location, he had to be prepared.

Apprehension plagued his soul when he thought about his mate betraying him. It was just like fate to give him hope then ruthlessly rip it from his claws before he could taste it. Rory huffed in frustration then paused. He heard a distant noise, heavy footsteps, as if someone was being chased. Rory looked out the window and it was her, his mate and she was running back to the cottage like hellfire. "Shite." He had to hide, but where? The place was so small and open. Acting on pure instinct Rory dashed behind the door and readied himself for an attack right before it burst open.

To his surprise his mate rushed in and frantically looked around the cottage, confused. *Aye, lass, ye thought ye had me right where ye wanted me,* he mused to himself as he held the knife in his hand and crouched down, ready to make his move like a hunter stalking his prey.

Chapter Five

With speed and courage she never realized she possessed, Kenna ran through the flames and barreled through the door to her cottage. Skidding to a halt, she was surprised she hadn't gone up in flames. Where were the flames? They were gone...vanished.

Once inside, the cottage appeared to be untarnished, undisturbed, as if the fire had never existed. What was happening? There was no denying she had seen her cottage on fire. As she searched the room, expecting to see some evidence of scorched walls or thatch, she scanned the floor where the wounded man should be lying. He was gone. "Where did he go?"

The door slammed shut and her head jerked towards it, then she felt ice cold steel against her throat and a warm body pressed against hers, restraining her from fleeing.

"I be right here, lass." The deep rich tone of his voice sent a shiver of fear down her spine, yet warmed her in places that weren't proper. Mistake number one: *Kenna, you forgot to tie him up.*

"Who are ye and why did ye try to kill me?" His warm breath wafted across her ear as his lips pressed against her. So he was the dragon after all.

"I will tell ye nothin', dragon," she gritted out through her teeth. With all her might, she stomped her boot down on Rory's bare foot.

"Shite!" Rory cried out and grabbed his foot, losing his grip around her neck.

Kenna quickly swung around and skittered backwards until the back of her legs hit her small bed behind her. Her legs buckled and down she went, sitting hard on the heather mattress. Right now she wished her cottage had more space.

Regaining his balance, Rory straightened. "Ye dinnae have to go and do that," he huffed in pain.

"I most certainly did. I'm tired of ye coming around here, setting blazes around me home."

Rory's brows furrowed in confusion. "Ye think I set that fire?"

Kenna crossed her arms over her chest and stiffened her chin. "Aye, I do."

"Och, lass, I didnae set those flames, in fact the flames are what brought me here to ye. I thought ye may be in danger."

Danger? Kenna thought. The mere fact that this man thought himself to be her hero agitated her. She didn't

39

need to be rescued when the only danger that threatened her was the dragon standing in front of her—naked. An uncomfortable awkwardness settled between them as Kenna looked anywhere but down.

A giggle escaped her, not because of the man's physique, but because she found it humorous to be arguing with a naked man.

"What?" Rory threw his hands in the air.

Kenna looked down at the man's length then back up at him through her long dark eyelashes, blushing.

"God's teeth!" Hurriedly Rory bent over, slightly brushing Kenna's arm as he reached for something to cover himself. Quickly he wrapped a blanket around his waist. "Please forgive me." He bowed his head. "Me name is Rory Cameron. Aye, I am a dragon and I mean ye no harm. I hope I can say the same aboot ye."

With Rory standing so close to her, half-dressed, she was rendered speechless. Try as she may to ignore the fact that her heart was racing so fast she could feel it pulsating through every vein in her body. No matter how hard she tried, she couldn't ease that terrible throbbing sensation occurring deep inside her every time he spoke.

She swallowed hard when she met his smoldering dark eyes. "Me name is Kenna Mackenzie." She wiped her sweaty hands down her trews before she offered her hand. "I'm terribly sorry for wounding ye."

Rory shrugged his shoulders then winced. "I'll be fine." He swayed and Kenna shot up from the bed to help him balance.

"Ye lost a lot of blood. Ye should be lying down." She helped him back to his pallet on the floor. He moaned in pain as he stretched out. "Let me help ye." Gently she held his head as he slowly took his time lying down on his back. "I have herbs here that will take away yer pain." She covered him with a blanket then stood.

"That would be most appreciated." He swallowed hard through the pain.

On her way to the kitchen she stopped and collected the purple leaves she had dropped. She placed them on the wooden table on her way to pour water into the cauldron. Heading back to the table she started crushing the leaves into a paste, pondering what Rory had said about the flames. If he wasn't the one causing them, who was? The flames always occurred when she ventured too far from her cottage, but never had they come close, let alone consumed her home and then disappeared. Mayhap there was some kind of magic here. The Fae were probably at their tricks again.

Once she was satisfied with the consistency of the paste, she scooped it into a bowl and gathered up some long strips of cloth. Before going back to where Rory lay, she ladled some hot water into a bowl. Bending down beside him, she untied the belt she'd used to stop the bleeding and unwrapped the blood-soaked bandages. How could she have been so brutal? The arrow had gone straight through his shoulder, barely missing the bone. She grabbed a cloth and dipped it into the hot water. "This might sting a wee bit," she warned.

Rory hissed overdramatically, which made Kenna jerk. She felt horrible that he was in so much pain. "This will be over soon. I need to clean the dirt from yer wound."

"Mayhap if ye blow on it, it might no' sting as much," Rory suggested.

"Aye." *Of course that would help.* She bent down and lightly blew across the wound. She swore she heard the man purr like an overgrown kitten.

Next she applied the purple paste over the wound and wrapped it. "There, ye should be feelin' better soon." She sat back and rested on her heels, pushing a strand of hair behind her ear.

Rory attempted to sit up and winced when he use the arm. "I think I might have wrenched it." He rubbed his arm as if he was trying to ease the pain.

Rory gained enough strength and kneeled down in front of Kenna. Even on his knees, he towered over her. Heat radiated from his body, warming her like sun rays beaming down on her skin. Quickly distracting herself from staring at his masculine physique, Kenna fumbled with a long, wide strip of cloth. "Here." Carefully bracing his elbow in her hand, she gently bent his arm in front of his chest, "Hold yer arm just like this. I'm going to wrap it in a sling." She then took the cloth lengthwise, placing his arm in the middle, cradled like a newborn babe. Hesitantly she moved closer, keeping her eyes on him at all times. As she tied the cloth behind his neck, Rory bent his head, assisting in her efforts. His warm breath brushed alongside her neck as if he was smelling her hair. The puff of air caused her to shiver.

"Lass, ye smell divine," he whispered into her ear.

Kenna froze, but her insides were fluttering out of control like a million butterflies released at once. She slid her hand down from around his neck, stopping at his chest as she sat back on her heels. Avoiding all contact, she stared down into her lap, fidgeting with her fingers.

"I have made ye uncomfortable, Kenna. I should probably be on my way. Thank ye for helping me with me wound."

He smiled and her proper thinking ceased. Something beyond desire, beyond lust told her not to let this man leave. She couldn't explain it, she felt it.

"Are ye hungry?" she asked, biting her bottom lip nervously. "'Tis no' a bother. I dinnae get many guests and I feel horrible for what I've done to ye. Let me at least feed ye."

Rory smiled. "Aye, lass."

Kenna stood. "Good, ye rest while I cook." She smiled then headed to the big black cauldron hanging over the hearth.

~~~~~

Rory relaxed into the soft furs with the taste of victory on his tongue. It had never tasted so good. He grinned. There weren't enough demons in hell to drag him away from Kenna. *Kenna Mackenzie.* Her name felt like a fine wine, smooth with a wee bit of spice. By the way she'd taken him in and tended to his wounds, she meant him no harm. Thank the Gods that be she wasn't a threat.

Mayhap not a threat as an enemy, however it was good she did not know how dangerous she truly was. It did puzzle him that she hadn't perceived him as her mate right away, not that he was familiar with all the rules that came along with finding a mate, or had experience in courting one. There was one factor that drove him forward; no matter how many rules he had to break to make Kenna realize he was her soul's mate, he was willing to crush each one until every boundary crumbled away.

Delicate, yet strong… vibrant, yet a lady… alluring, yet shrewd—Kenna was more than he could ever have hoped for in a female. She never once batted an eyelash when he confirmed his dragon side. He exhaled. Aye, he had to tread softly or else he could ruin his chances with her, because he had no intention of leaving anytime soon.

Certainly he felt bad for exaggerating his reactions to the wound, but he had to do something to ensure his stay. Aye, he had walked a fine line when he suggested leaving, taking the gamble nonetheless. However, it was working in his favor, because there was no way Kenna would turn away a helpless wounded man, unless he was an eejit and crossed the line physically, which he had almost done.

His wound was healing rapidly. Actually, by the time they had reached the cottage, it had started to close up. With a careful eye on Kenna, he had reopened the bloody injury twice. But it paid off nicely as he watched Kenna preparing their meal. Rory growled as she dipped her index finger in the stew broth she had been stirring, then licked the juices from her finger. Bloody hell, he wished he was sucking on that slender finger of hers. Kenna glanced over at him and smiled. She must have heard his growl.

"Sounds to me ye must be verra hungry," she said as she diced some carrots.

Rory returned her smile. "Aye, verra." If only she knew how famished he was.

Kenna placed the knife down and went over to the pot hanging above the fire. Rory watched her wrap her long, slender fingers around the handle of a ladle. The beast groaned. He yearned to feel those fingers gripped around his cock, pleasuring him.

With his resolve hanging on by a fraying thread, Rory needed to be a good dragon and mind his manners, but Kenna was too intoxicating. Everything about her mesmerized him.

As if Rory wasn't being tortured enough, Kenna bent over to adjust the firewood. The leather trews that hugged her arse nicely left nothing to the imagination.

45

Rory fisted the furs, resisting the temptation to go to the lass and bury himself in her treasures.

After a few more perilous moments, during which Rory's self-control was sorely tested, Kenna finished setting the table and called him over for supper.

He wrapped a blanket around his waist, adjusting himself, careful not to reveal how much he desired the lass. Deftly playing the role of the poor newly injured, Rory slowly made his way to the table, pulling out a chair for Kenna. She took her seat as he sat across from her. Without hesitation or waiting for Kenna to take the first bite, Rory leaned over his bowl of stew and inhaled the savory aroma. Resting his arms around his supper as if he was a dog guarding its meal, he plunged in, shoveling a big spoonful of broth and vegetables into his mouth. The flavorful mixture awakened his tongue and drew him in for another taste. Assaulting the wooden bowl greedily until he sensed her eyes on him, he looked up from his bowl and met Kenna's stoic gaze. Backing away from the damage he had done to the stew, Rory retreated and wiped his mouth.

"Either ye be really hungry or me cookin' be to yer likin'," Kenna said as she tore off a hunk of bread and reluctantly handed it to him, retracting her hand quickly as if he would bite her.

Evidently he found his manners and chewed and swallowed a hunk of carrot before answering her. "Och, lass, yer cookin' is fit for a king. Excuse me poor manners."

"'Tis fine." With her elbows off the table, Kenna picked up her spoon, scooped up some stew, and then delicately blew on it before putting it in her mouth.

Ah, his mate had a proper side.

Avoiding eye contact, Kenna looked down into her bowl, swirling her spoon around the edges of it. "I dinnae usually have guests. 'Tis me pleasure to cook for ye."

"The next time ye want to have a guest over for supper, ye might no' want to shoot him oot of the sky," he teased.

Kenna snickered. "I suppose ye're right."

"Though I must ask, where did ye get all these weapons from? I've never seen anything like them."

"I made them."

"Ye? How?"

"Aye." Kenna placed her spoon on the table neatly next to her bowl then picked up a tankard filled with wine. She pulled from it like she hadn't drunk for days. She set the wine down and licked her lips. Rory swore he was going to go up in flames. He would have sold his soul to assist her in licking the wine from those plump lips. "'Tis hard to explain. An image comes to me, then my body takes over until I finish my creation. Sometimes days pass before I realize it."

"And the weapon ye used on me?"

47

"Och, ye mean Dragon Slayer?"

Rory arched a dark brow. "Dragon Slayer?"

Kenna took another long pull of wine before answering. "I...I thought the only creature big enough to set the flames I've seen would be a dragon. So, my last invention was inspired by—" She shrugged her shoulders. "Ye know the story."

"Aye, I dinnae blame ye for wanting to defend yer home." Rory popped a hunk of bread in his mouth.

"Now 'tis my turn, *dragon*," she said with emphasis on the last word. "I didnae know humans could..." She paused to think of a word that would best describe his attributes. "Become dragons. In all honesty, I've seen me share of creatures, but nothing like... you."

"What kind of creatures?" Rory asked, not wanting to answer her question, for his Kine was complicated, and it was too early to explain it all.

Kenna leaned forward. "Ye be skirting around me question, beastie. But if ye must know, the Fae."

"Aye, careful of those flighty tricksters. Not only can they be a pain in the arse, but if approached the wrong way, they can be deadly vengeful beings."

Kenna shot him a cross stare.

"Fine." Defeated, Rory put down his spoon and cleared his throat. "Let me clarify one small detail. Not just any human can shift into a dragon. I come from a long line of noble dragon elders on the male side, of course. We are our own race, called Dragonkine. 'Tis really complicated to explain, Kenna." Rory hoped that she would cease her questioning, for he didn't want to reveal the awakening of Drest, their king, nor the destruction that would come to the Kine if he and his brothers-in-arms didn't pledge their loyalty to their Dragon King. His commander had already made it crystal clear he should confirm his stance and continue to stay true to Robert the Bruce, King of Scotland. Rory had been the only one to fly off, not pledging his loyalty either way.

War was coming, and he had to make a decision, one that would change his life forever. Join Drest and destroy the human race or refuse to join, and become one of Drest's victims.

"Rory?"

Shaken from his thoughts, he brought his attention back to Kenna.

"I asked ye aboot female dragons?"

Thankful for the distraction, Rory rubbed the tension from the back of his neck. "Nay, no female dragons, but there are female Dragonkine, our mates." He paused, not knowing how far to take the mating issue. "Kenna, our race was demolished centuries ago, back in the time of King MacAlpin. My Kine had females we could no' live without. They calmed our dragon side and made us whole. When MacAlpin attacked our kingdom, our

49

females went into hiding. For the longest time we thought they were dead."

The amazing thing about finding one's mate was how in tune one became with their emotions, and Rory felt every stinging bit of Kenna's torment on his behalf. She was speechless.

"Though as of late, a few of my brethren have found their mates to be human." Rory shrugged this information off fast, spooning stew into his mouth.

Taken aback, Kenna retreated, bewildered. "Rory, I'm so terribly sorry. 'Tis tragic."

He nodded his head, chewing. "Aye." He drank some wine to wash down his meal. "Now, my turn. Why are ye oot here all alone?"

All at once frantic scratches came from outside the door. "Finn." Kenna jumped out of her chair and ran to let the gray wolf inside.

Rory smirked to himself. The wolf had impeccable timing.

As soon as Kenna opened the door, Finn ran inside and instantly shook, launching droplets of water everywhere. "Ah, Finn!" Kenna threw her hands up to block a shower of water. "Oh laddie, I be so sorry. I didnae know it was raining outside."

As Rory finished eating, he took in the scene. It was downright impossible not to chuckle at the way she talked and catered to her wolf. The gray beast pushed against her, drying himself on her trews. At that moment, Rory realized how intimidating this beast was. However, the wolf was a playful pup in Kenna's hands; a companion like no other. Jealousy reared its ugly head when his mate kneeled down to Finn's level and scratched him behind the ears. He'd never seen a smile so genuine, so pure. It was as if he was drawn to her beauty like a moth to flame. He couldn't resist staring at her with wonder and utter delight that this feisty, good-natured lass was his. How could one dragon be so lucky? *Ah, but Rory Cameron, dinnae count yer blessing before yer destiny has been fulfilled.*

Kenna stood, straightening her hair as Finn took his place next to the hearth, warming his body from the cold rain. "Rory, this be Finn."

"Och, Finn looks like a fine lad."

Kenna sat at the table, gleefully glancing at the wolf. "Aye, he's the finest. I rescued him five years ago. Ye should have seen how pitiful he was. I had me doubts aboot his wounds. They were verra deep."

"Finn is lucky to have ye." Rory smiled, winking his dimples at her.

Some time passed and silence filled the space between them as the fire in the hearth cracked and snapped. The warm orange glow created a cozy atmosphere throughout the cottage as the dark gray rainclouds settled above the glen. The weapons danced together as a loud burst of thunder shook the cottage, followed by jagged lines of lightning separating the night sky. Rain as heavy as stones pelted the thatched roof and the wind howled an eerie tune.

Rory studied Kenna's face—worry blended with fright. "Lass, looks as if I'll be staying the night."

Chapter Six

Five years was a long time to hold on to hope, to unwaveringly seek out the truth, to have the patience one needs in the sure and certain knowledge one always gets what one wants. Those were the words of wisdom Ian Mackintosh had lived by ever since his bride had gone missing. Well, that was what he told his people, because no lass in her right state of mind would flee from him and abandon the title of Lady Mackintosh of Glenloch. It was a privilege, a noble duty, the dream of many women. So why had Kenna left him?

To this day, Ian traveled from village to village, accompanied by a fierce band of Clan Mackintosh men. From the outside looking in, one would think, as they saw the men approaching, that it was strictly business as usual: time to pay rent. Whether one lived on Mackintosh land or needed their protection, it came with a price. But 'twas better to pay a fellow Highlander than a dirty *Sassenach*.

Ian kept his true intentions to himself. He did not have to do the Mackintosh business that forced him out on these daunting travels week after week, sometimes even month after month. The Laird of Glenloch and clan chief always had men lined up eager to do his bidding. But Ian had a secret reason—to find Kenna. He breathed, slept, and lived to find her, never giving up hope that one day he would bring her back home.

"My Laird, should we set up camp over there?" Samuel, one of his most loyal men pointed to a clearing in the village market.

The closer to the crowd the better, had always been Ian's motto when setting up camp. Like a hunter pursuing its prey, he dismounted and focused on where he should start searching for the lass with the long brown hair. "Aye, Samuel."

Tying his warhorse to a nearby tree, he walked over to a barrel outside a tavern that had been filled with fresh rainwater. He splashed the cool water on his face and the back of his neck, rubbing it to relieve the stiffness. Since the ride had been long and tiresome, Ian's muscles cried out and protested against his will to keep moving, he continued to search. Sleep would only take away time that could be spent searching for Kenna.

Ian splashed his face one last time, shaking off the excess water. A disturbance from the market square piqued his curiosity. He opened his eyes to a merchant arguing with a woman. A woman with a slender frame, a woman with long brown hair. Urgently, he wiped his face, trying to get a clearer view. If only he could see her face.

Running his fingers through his long blond bangs, he made his way to the square where merchants sold their goods and local townsfolk flocked. How busy one market would be depended on the size of the village. And today this market square was swarming, the busiest he had seen, which was good for him; rent would be paid in coin instead of trades.

The closer Ian got to the square the more crowded it became. In a rush to make it to the merchant before he lost sight of the woman, Ian shouldered his way through the crowd without paying attention and bumped right into a child, knocking her to the ground.

"Och, lass." Ian bent down and helped the child to her feet. "Ye be well?"

The red-headed, freckle-faced child looked up at him. Her face turned red with anger and she kicked him in the shin. "Ye should mind where ye're goin'," she huffed and stormed away, leaving Ian clutching his shin and cursing silently. "Impudent child!" he groaned.

Shaking off the pain, he continued to dodge and slide between people until at last he reached the merchant's table. "The woman that was here with the long brown hair, where did she go?"

The merchant looked at him with furrowed brows.

Ian grabbed the man by his tunic and pulled him close. "Where did she go?"

"I…I…do no' know," the merchant stuttered.

Disgusted with the man, Ian pushed him back and let go of his tunic. In frustration Ian ran his fingers through his hair.

He spun around, frantically searching the crowd for the mystery woman. As he was about to move on, he caught a glimpse of her about to turn the corner down a dirt path between the cordwainer and the fletcher's shop. She peered over her cloak-clad shoulder and smiled at him. Ian's heart plummeted. It was Kenna.

The crowd of people multiply by the second as Ian fought his way toward his fiancée. "Kenna!" he yelled, looking over the masses. Reaching a wooden sign with a carved arrow on it, he realized he had reached the fletcher's shop. She had to be close.

Persistence drove him farther down the pathway between the two shops. Turning the corner, he rushed forward, closing the distance between them. He reached out to grab Kenna's shoulder, but was still too far away. This was it, the moment he had dreamed of many times over—he had found his Kenna.

No matter what her reason for leaving him on their wedding day, Ian did not care. Kenna was and would always be the love of his life. Indeed, he was aware of her concerns about fitting into his world—scrutinizing eyes followed her everywhere she went. Clan Mackintosh were a sanctimonious clan in their own right—neither showing loyalty to the King of Scotland, nor the King of England, they lived by their own rules and regulations, which served them well, since clans from all around the land came seeking protection under the Mackintosh name. When Ian brought an outsider into their tight trusted circle, the whole clan watched with suspicion. 'Twas not proper for a man of his birth to fall in love with his mother's lady's maid. In a way, Ian didn't blame her for leaving.

He spun the woman around. She faced Ian abruptly and slowly revealed her identity. A sinister laugh poured from her mouth, sending a chill down his spine. Long brown hair transformed to gray straggled strands. Flawless youthful skin now wrinkled and auld covered her body. The woman pointed a boney, crooked finger at the distressed Mackintosh laird. "Ye will never find her," the auld crone taunted and cackled.

Ian stood dumbfounded, then quickly became enraged. He'd seen Kenna. What had this auld hag done to her? "Crone, I'll have ye sent to the gallows if ye dinnae tell me what ye have done with Kenna." Approaching the woman as if he were going to shake the answer out of her, he reached for her shoulders. His forceful hands slipped straight through her. She was gone, leaving Ian stunned and confused.

Desperately he turned in circles, stubbornly searching for the woman. How could this be? He'd seen Kenna with his own eyes. *How does one vanish into thin air?*

Ian surrendered and leaned against the side of the shoemaker's shop. The chill of the stone wall bit into his back, welcoming the coolness on his skin. He slammed his head twice against the stone. When would this nightmare end?

His knees buckled from the weight of it all and he slid down the wall, hitting his arse on the ground with a thud. He drew his knees up and rested his arms on them. He hung his head low between his legs—the picture of a defeated man.

A defeated man he might be, but he would never give up on Kenna.

"My Laird!" Ian looked up to see hefty Samuel sprinting down the pathway toward him as if he had something important to say.

Hunched over, resting his hands on his thighs, Samuel sucked in much needed air. "My Laird…ye are…needed back at camp."

Brows furrowed, Ian demanded, "And what might this dire need for my return be?"

"'Tis Kenna's uncle. He's here and says he has something urgent to discuss wit' ye."

Ian flew to his feet. He didn't know whether to run back to camp anxiously like a wee lass falling in love for the first time or stay here, frozen from the thought that something terrible could have happened to Kenna. He placed his hands on his hips as he thought long and hard about what to do next. The auld woman had left him uneasy and shaken.

"Samuel, did her uncle give any indication of the urgency?"

"Nay, My Laird."

Ian sternly brushed back his long blond hair and made his way down the pathway with lengthy imperative strides, heading back to camp, all the way pondering what the emergency might be.

A huge blue and white, thick striped tent had been prepared for collecting rent. About twenty townsfolk stood in a single file line outside the opening, waiting to pay their share for Mackintosh protection. Ian shouldered his way into the tent, demanding everyone leave except Kenna's uncle.

Kenneth had his back turned with an authoritative hand on his hip. Once the two of them were alone he turned to face Ian with a smug smile. "I have found her."

Ian's heart flipped and plunged into his stomach. "Are ye sure? Where is she? We must leave now." Ian strode to the tent's opening, ready to head the search.

"Hold on, Ian. We must tread softly. There's one small obstacle in our way."

Ian halted and stood still. "And what may that be?" he asked over his shoulder.

"For weeks now I've been following an auld gypsy woman into the Great Glen. I found it odd that she was taking supplies into the woods, so I followed her. There's a cottage surround by some kind of...magic."

Remembering his unusual encounter with an auld woman, Ian gradually turned to face Kenneth. "An auld gypsy woman?"

59

"Aye."

"And what does this have to do wit' Kenna?"

A grim expression came over Kenneth's face as he swallowed past the lump in his throat. "The auld woman came upon a clearing in the glen. She waved her hands in front of her and a cottage appeared oot of thin air. I saw Kenna greet the auld crone and welcome her inside. When the woman left, the cottage, it…it vanished."

Ian advanced on Kenneth and grabbed his tunic. "If this be some kind of trickery, I'll see yer head upon a spike," he growled.

Stuttering, Kenneth pleaded, "'Tis no trickery. I know what I saw."

Loosening his grip, Ian took a step back and regained his composure.

Although Kenneth had no reason to lie to him, Ian had to guard his heart. He had been on too many dead end searches throughout the years. Those memories tore at his longing to find his runaway bride. How much more false hope could he withstand? How much more could his heart take before it was too late and he had nothing more to give? This had to be it…it had to.

A clap of thunder shook the tent and the wind howled, blowing the flaps of the opening inside. The air chilled him. Kenna might have escaped him tonight, but they would be reunited soon.

"We leave at daybreak. Ye'll lead the way," Ian commanded. The irritation in his voice was clear and Kenneth didn't dare to argue.

Ian quit camp and found himself in search of a tavern. A dram or two of ale would calm his restless soul for the night, for this night would be the longest he had ever endured. All he could think about was his reunion with Kenna.

Victoria Zak

Chapter Seven

"There." Kenna stepped back from the long fur she'd hung, dividing the space between her and Rory's sleeping areas. She blew a loose strand of brown hair from her face and placed her hands on her hips, viewing the wall. "This should give us some privacy." She turned to face Rory, who was lying down on his pallet next to the hearth, with Finn.

"If ye say so. Though ye might catch a chill since the fire is on my side." He winked and nodded his head toward the flames.

Kenna glared at him crossly, but there was playfulness in her tone. "Dragon, if ye think ye can trick me into yer bed, ye be terribly mistaken."

Rory placed his unwounded hand on his heart. "I love it when ye call me dragon, lass."

Kenna shook her head, smiling as she pulled back the wall of fur and disappeared behind it. "Good night…dragon." Snickering inwardly, she knew very well she was playing with fire when an escaped growl coming from the other side of the wall released a flutter within her.

Lying down on her bed with a heavy, exhausted sigh, Kenna stared at the ceiling, trying to forget the smolder in Rory's dark eyes and the fullness of his lips when he smiled at her. And if that wasn't wicked enough, the man had dimples that always appeared to wink at her. Kenna huffed and rolled over, clenching her pillow. Aye, there would be no sweet slumber tonight.

Shutting her eyes, she took in a deep breath and was trying to get some rest when she heard Rory rustling around—a perpetual reminder that a naked, virile man was right outside that fur wall. Or was it the constant ache betwixt her legs that kept her awake? She tightened her thighs as she recalled the moment when she'd first seen Rory in all his masculine glory. His body must have been carved by the Gods, for no human man had muscles in places where Rory had. "Maiden, mother crone," she whispered under her breath.

"Kenna?" Her heart skipped, hearing her name on his lips. Had she been thinking out loud? She cleared her throat. "Aye."

"Are ye awake?"

Kenna rolled onto her back. "Aye."

"I hate to be a bother, but me shoulder is verra painful."

Kenna exhaled, relieved she had kept her thoughts to herself. "I'll be right there." She sat up and swung her legs over the edge of the bed. She'd been too distracted with the dragon and forgotten to take her boots off. Just as well, since the floor was probably cold.

Straightening her clothes and taking a deep breath, she drew back the corner of the fur and peeked out. The air froze in her lungs. He looked as if he was a golden god as he lay there on her floor, glowing from the fire casting a warm orange hue across his bare chest. Her gaze slid down farther, taking in every inch of him until his nakedness disappeared under the woolen blanket. Beads of sweat dotted her upper lip.

Rory sat up, concerned. "Are ye well?"

"Aye." Kenna looked away, trying to conceal her blushing cheeks as she came out from hiding and scurried past Rory to the kitchen. She made her way to the herb shelf full of jars and took the self-heal, then headed back to Rory. "Where does it hurt?" she asked, holding his dark stare.

"Right here." He pushed the top of the sling down and pointed to his shoulder.

"Does it feel like muscle pain?"

"Aye."

Kenna kneeled down in front of him and rubbed her hands together to suppress the cold. Her body tensed under his searing, hot gaze as she reached into the jar, grabbing a handful of purple paste. They locked eyes before she smeared the self-heal on his aching muscles. "This won't hurt," she reassured him.

She felt comfortable around Rory. There was an ease about him that made her crave his company. Perhaps it was the way he jested or the way he scratched Finn behind the ears. Whatever it might be, she liked it.

Focusing on Rory's sore shoulder, Kenna settled her nerves. She pressed the palms of her hands deep against his skin, massaging the muscles with her thumbs in a circular motion.

"Lass, do ye normally wear yer boots to bed?" Rory asked, and snapped the top of her boot against her leg.

Kenna chuckled. "Nay, I forgot to take them off."

"'Tis no' every day I come across a lass dressed in men's clothing."

She felt his subjective gaze examining her attire. "Have ye ever hunted in skirts before?" She raised a cross brow at him.

"Nay," he chuckled, "I suppose I haven't."

"I dinnae get many visitors, so I wear what's comfortable. I'm sorry if I have offended ye."

"Nay, lass, dinnae be sorry." Rory took her long, thick braid in his hands and caressed its silken strands. "I'll never look at a pair of trews the same way ever again."

Kenna blushed and teased back, "'Tis no' proper to speak to a lady like that."

"Och, now look who's offending who," he scoffed and released her braid.

Kenna slipped the sling back up onto Rory's shoulder when the last of the paste had been absorbed. "Now," she sat back on her heels, "how does it feel?"

"'Tis good." He smiled and readjusted the sling.

Kenna stayed and held his gaze longer than her common sense told her she should. Wise reasoning warned her to leave while she still had the nerve, yet it battled fiercely with her womanly instincts to stay and explore this Highlander a wee bit longer. Rory's heated gaze mesmerized her, scorching her soul. Aye, she had stayed longer than she should have. There was something hidden deep within his dark eyes, something that felt familiar. Something that felt right.

Embarrassed for staring, she broke away and cleared her throat. "I should let ye rest." She was about to leave, but Rory grabbed her wrist. She stared at his hand, then locked eyes with him. "Would it be improper if I wanted to kiss ye?" Rory filled the empty space between them and leaned in closer.

Taking in the fullness of his mouth, Kenna innocently licked her lips. A primal growl rumbled in the back of Rory's throat, sending liquid heat rushing through her veins. *Aye, it is improper!* It was improper for an unmarried woman to have a man, naked to boot, in her home without an escort. Aye, it was improper to be

66

lustful over a man who she did not know. Aye, she knew better than to trust a dragon.

She pressed her lips together and thought carefully how to address the situation. Even though proper wasn't a word that often described her, she was still a lady with good morals in regards to her pure virtues. "Aye, it would be verra---" Before she could finish the thought, Rory leaned in and claimed her lips for his own. There was no sweet and subtle, no testing the ground before he went in for the kill. With Rory it was all or nothing.

With every lick he drew her in deeper until all her reservations melted away and there was only Rory. Their tongues danced to a seductive tune only they could hear. Capturing the back of Kenna's neck, he pulled her closer, deepening the kiss. The sensation of hot embers pricked her skin as she felt her need for him grow stronger. If she didn't excuse herself now and run and hide under her furs, undoubtedly she would be inclined to do something improper.

Although she would regret it, her good morals got the best of her. She placed her hands on his chest and tenderly pushed him away, breaking their kiss. She looked up at him through her dark eyelashes and caught her breath. "I bid ye a good night." Quickly she found her footing and strode back behind the comfort of the wall of furs.

~~~~~

Sexual frustration was not a problem that often plagued Rory, however last night it had taken all his resolve not to tear down that damn wall and lay to rest the ache in his cock. Honeysuckle still lingered as he licked the flavor from his lips—a flavor he would not soon forget. One taste of Kenna left him itching for more, a fixation he could not ignore, nor did he want to.

The fire in the hearth had gone out, indicating he must have dozed off sometime during the early morning hours. Even though his injury seemed fully healed, a dragon needed a deep sleep to heal completely. Furthermore, he needed to keep his healing ability a secret a bit longer until Kenna was ready to accept him as her mate. By the way she had opened up to him last night, he sensed it wouldn't be much longer.

Rory exhaled. "Bloody hell." The thought of being mated hit him square in the chest. As he lay there on the floor, absorbed in his inner musing, an old feeling crept inside, taunting him to run…run far away and never look back. The old Rory would never stand for settling with one woman. The old Rory never fell in love; it was all about sex, nothing more. His dragon stirred from deep inside and growled, letting him know he was a fool for thinking of the past.

He sat up and ran his fingers through his disheveled hair. "Aye, beastie, I hear ye."

What he needed more than anything right now was a dip in the loch to cool off, and food in his belly. He was surprised that the rumbling hadn't woken Kenna. Since the cottage was still quiet, he had enough time to make it to the loch and back before Kenna woke and, hopefully, prepare something to break their fast.

Not having his own clothes, Rory grabbed a plaid from a nearby chair and wrapped it around his waist. A bit small, but it would make do for his short jaunt down to the loch. Not wanting to wake Kenna, he slipped out the door without disturbing a soul.

Gray clouds had stayed behind from last night's storm and residual rain collected in droplets on every tree leaf. Nothing felt better to him than the cool misty morning breeze after a rainstorm. It was as if the rain washed away the old and left behind the newness of a fresh day. He inhaled, taking in the woodsy smell of the glen and…honeysuckle? Rory furrowed his brows as he heard splashing coming from the loch.

Quietly, he crouched down and snuck along the path leading to the loch. Once he saw what was making the splashing noise he hid behind a thick rowan tree and peeked around it to the loch. He grinned like a lad who had snuck an oatcake from underneath his mother's nose as he watched Kenna dip into the water and back up again. Long brown hair cascaded down her back and glistened. If only she would turn around so he could feast his eyes on her full beauty. Rory found himself tightening his grip on the tree. Claws extended, he dug deeper into the bark when she dove underwater, exposing her full, round arse cheeks. "Holy hell," he whispered. He clenched his length, attempting to relieve the constant throb, but it was pointless. There was only one way to release the ache—to be inside Kenna.

A branch snapped under his foot. Finn, who had been drinking at the water's edge, perked his head up, looking right at him. Shite, he had stayed too long. If he was a gentleman he would have left her to her privacy. Alas for Kenna, he had never claimed to be one.

Startled by Finn's unexpected departure, Kenna turned around and dipped into the loch neck deep. "Who's there?"

Out from behind the rowan tree Rory and Finn walked to the water's edge. "I thought I would join ye." Rory began to unwrap the plaid.

"Absolutely not! Ye stay out of this water, Rory. I mean it!" Kenna replied sharply.

Rory had never experienced rejection before, especially not from a lass. Taken aback, this one stung. After last night's kiss why wouldn't she want him to join her? Had he read her wrong? Perhaps being too forward had cost him one step back in the wrong direction. Christ, what he wouldn't do right now to be in that loch licking those droplets from her skin. If she didn't want him in the loch with her, then he would make her come to him.

She stuck her arm out of the water and pointed to a nearby fallen tree. "Hand me my shift."

Rory picked it up and showed it to her. "Ye mean this?"

Kenna rolled her eyes. "Aye."

"Well, lass, there seems to be a problem." Rory strolled to the edge of the water in front of her. "Ye told me to stay out of the water. If ye want it ye'll have to come and get it," he smirked.

Rory expected her to bark back, indicating that she would rather freeze than expose her naked body to him. But he couldn't have been more wrong. In fact, what she did left him speechless and that didn't happened very often.

Kenna squared her shoulders and locked eyes with him as she emerged from the water, crossing her arms over her breasts to preserve some of her dignity. Her slick, wet body was completely exposed to him all the way down to her toes. Rory begged for time to stand still, for her body was beyond beautiful. His hands itched to touch her flawless, peachy skin and his mouth watered, wanting to taste every delectable inch of her.

Kenna now stood so close to him that he could hear the droplets of water falling into the sand, collecting in pools by her feet. There was a look in her eyes that he couldn't quite figure out. Was it hatred? Was it disappointment? Was it lust?

After making him sweat trying to figure out what she was going to do to him, Kenna held her arm out carefully, keeping the other one across her breasts. "Me shift," she said too calmly for Rory's liking.

He handed her the shift.

Without saying a word, she wrapped the sheer material around her body, holding it in place behind her back. It stuck to her like a second skin. Rory watched Kenna as she strolled past him as if his seeing her naked meant nothing to her. She sauntered over to the pathway leading back to the cottage then looked over her shoulder at him. "'Tis no' proper for a man to watch a woman's backside as she walks away." She smiled and loosened her grip on her shift, exposing her finest asset.

Thunderstruck and completely amazed that he'd met his match, Rory stood motionless. He couldn't believe this woman was his mate.

He watched her until she vanished through the thickness of the glen. With the image of Kenna's arse forever embedded in his mind, he tossed the plaid and ran into the loch, splashing as he dove into the coolness. It was going to take more than a quick dip to ease his urge to bury himself deep within Kenna's treasure.

Chapter Eight

Once back at the cottage, Kenna slammed the door shut behind her and rested her back against it. She covered her mouth and held back an enthusiastic giggle while her heart raced like a fleeing hare's.

Drop-jawed and stunned, the confounded expression on Rory's face had been worth the possible repercussions. With the flicker of shamelessness swirling in those dark eyes, she knew she might very well be in over her head. Surely Kenna had never been forward toward a man like that before, exposing her nakedness, yet his jesting and trickery brought out her mischievous side. Provoking Rory turned out to be more delightful than she could ever have imagined. He had toyed with her long enough; she wanted to make him squirm for a change. Aye, she had played with fire and she prayed she would feel the burn.

After she dressed in her normal attire, leather trews, tunic, and fitted jerkin that tied up the front, Kenna donned her boots and sat on her bed thinking about how she was going to keep him out of the cottage. In close proximity she most definitely didn't trust herself around him. Fresh air, green grass, and lying under the blue sky would give her plenty of room to breathe. A sound plan indeed.

Kenna grabbed a basket and filled it with bread. The morn had not showed signs of a sun-filled day, but that wasn't going to stop her from breaking their fast outside. There was a spot, her favorite; a cliff overlooking the moor and full of cloudberries, which would be a delicious addition to the bread. Instead of waiting for Rory's return, Kenna headed to her favorite spot. If she was guessing right, he would find her with no problem.

In no time she picked enough berries, laid out a blanket, and sat looking across the moor, waiting. At this time of year heather grew to its fullest, stippling the land with purple flowers. Often she came here to reflect and hoped for a vision to reveal what lay ahead, however the future of her unborn son was still a mystery. Firm in her resolve never to return to Glenloch, she couldn't help but think about how her life would have changed if she had been honest and told Ian everything.

Her heart grew heavy thinking about her auld life. Normally she didn't allow herself to think of the past—it only brought her heartache. Even though she didn't particularly enjoy being the center of attention around Ian and his clan, she missed socializing with the few friends who hadn't viewed her with critical eyes and had allowed her to be herself and not Ian Mackintosh's lady.

As the heather swayed back and forth, dancing in the wind, she had all but forgotten how she loved to dance to the tin whistle. Back home, a group of traveling musicians would come to town, playing tunes she had never heard before. The music crept into her soul from the first time she'd encountered the mesmerizing harmonies. Unaware of her feet tapping to the beat, she fancied a dance.

Although it pleased Ian to see her happy and alive while she danced with the crowd, he would never join her, because Lady Mackintosh disapproved. *A clan chief must be viewed as a resilient warrior and well respected. No one honors a man who frolics around dancing like a fool.* Ian's reputation had been tarnished enough when he chose a lady's maid for betrothal. Forever haunted, Kenna could still feel the lady's stern, steel gray eyes on her. Whenever a shiver pricked her spine while she twirled to the music, she knew why. It was Kenna's clue that the dance was over.

She tucked those memories away when a new thought surfaced; her future. Hot breath panted across her face and a wet nose nudged her neck. "Finn." She made her best effort to smile at the gray wolf sitting beside her, but failed miserably. "Oh, Finn, what am I going to do?"

The wolf exhaled heavily in response to her distress.

"I know I need to tell him, but my heart tells me no' to." Again, just as she had five years ago, she sat heartbroken. The mere thought of sending Rory away opened up auld wounds, scars she wished she could hide. Foresight had warned her to stay away from Ian and now she had to hold firm, err on the side of caution and not take a husband, nor engage in the pleasures of a man. Not until she was positive her son would be honorable.

Kenna observed her wolf chivalrously perched next to her as he surveyed the moor. A pure sight of beauty and power. She ran her fingers through his fur, taking comfort in its softness. "Mayhap I could keep my secret a wee bit longer, aye?"

Finn turned his head and glared down his nose at her, then nudged her with a disapproving shove.

Defeated, Kenna exhaled. "I know. I have to tell him."

"Tell me what?" Rory bent down to greet Finn with an ear scratch.

Rory caught Kenna off-guard, for she hadn't heard him coming. Maiden, mother, crone... what was she going to do? More to the point, what could she possibly say?

Kenna swallowed past the lump in her throat. "I...I see ye found the trews and shirt I left for ye." *Coward!*

Finn snapped his head toward Kenna and growled low and deep, causing her to respond with a stern glower, sending a message loud and clear that her business didn't concern a certain wolf. Finn glared crossly, then took off into the glen.

Quickly Kenna skirted around the question. "I had a pair of men's trews that I hadn't altered. They fit ye perfectly." She regarded him up and down.

"Aye, thank ye." Rory sat down beside her and instantly she felt his heat. "Ye look far away, lass. What be on yer mind?"

How was it possible for a stranger to know her so well, as if they had met before? Or could dragons read minds? God she hoped not. *Kenna Mackenzie, pull yerself together!*

Kenna cleared her throat and disregarded Rory's query. "Are ye hungry?" She opened the basket and placed the bread on the plaid, unwrapping it from a cloth. "I have bread and berries." She took a berry in her hand and offered it to Rory, stopping abruptly when she met his glare.

Black brows were furrowed over black as night eyes, swirling with intensity. "Ye can tell me. I will no' pass judgment."

His smolder caused her to blink and avoid any more eye contact, because if she beheld those blazing pits she would lose all her will. She picked up a berry and picked at its skin. "I was merely thinking back to a time when my life wasn't so complicated."

"Complicated? Ye live in a cottage secluded in the woods. What could be so complicated aboot that?"

Kenna shook her head. "Do ye think I want to be here alone, Rory? Well, I do no'." To be rude was not in her nature, nor did she mean to sound so harsh. Furthermore, she hadn't realized how angry she had become. Years of pent-up frustration had gotten the best of her. She stood and dusted off her trews, then walked to the edge of the cliff, never taking her eyes off the serenity of the dancing heather below.

She rested her shoulder against a tree, crossing her arms in front of her as if she was shielding herself from further heartache. "All I wanted to do was dance." She hung her head and kicked a rock off the cliff.

When there was no response, Kenna glanced over her shoulder to see if Rory still sat on the blanket. She wouldn't blame him if he left; her mood had turned foul. To her surprise Rory stood behind her with his hand outstretched. "Would ye dance wit' me?"

Kenna remembered her mother warning her about lads and that love is a feeling you cannot describe unless you've experienced it. Butterfly wings fluttering out of control…fish flopping in the pit of your stomach…air ceasing to exist…it was all true. After one small act of kindness, every wise tale about love bloomed inside her when she held Rory's gaze.

"Ye can no' dance. Yer arm is injured. In fact ye should probably be resting it." Kenna pursued to sulk but stopped when Rory ripped the sling from his arm and threw it to the ground.

Shocked, she darted to pick it up. "What are ye doing? Have ye gone daft?"

"Nay. Lass, I've been healed since ye brought me back to yer cottage. A wee arrow can no' take down a dragon."

Kenna pressed her hand to her chest, not believing what she was hearing. "Ye pretended to be injured?"

"I…" Rory rubbed the back of his neck. "I only wanted yer attention. I meant ye no harm."

"Ye tricked me!" She kicked his shin.

"Ouch!" Rory grabbed his shin. "Hold on! Ye shot an arrow at me and ye're the one angry?"

Kenna crossed her arms and glared at Rory in silence. How could she have been so foolish as to believe him? Had loneliness made her gullible?

Rory held his hand out to her. "Truce?"

Kenna looked away and declined his peace offering.

He bent down to look her in the face, but she ignored him. "I promise, no more tricks." Rory again tried to gain at least one glance from her. "Kennnnaaaa. I'm a verra good dancer." Rory wobbled his knees together in an attempt at a jest.

Kenna covered her mouth with her hand to hold back the laughter that threatened to bubble over into hysterics. She didn't have the heart to stay mad at him, for he was making a complete fool out of himself for her sake.

Laughter burst from her until breathing became hard. "I do hope ye can dance better than that."

Rory stopped his knee jig and offered his hand. "Let me show ye."

She accepted and he guided her around him in an arm's length circle. When she dared to let go of his hand, Rory simply pulled her closer until their bodies were tightly pressed together. Caught off guard, Kenna wrapped her arms around his neck to steady herself, for if Rory wasn't holding her, she would surely float far into the clouds. He reached around his neck and took her hand, placing it on his heart. He dipped his head down until their foreheads touched with an intensity that heated Kenna from the inside out.

Peaceful contentment, unlike anything she'd felt before, surged through her and she closed her eyes, relishing his touch as they swayed to the tune of their hearts. No music, no distance between them, no analytical glares. Alone they lived in the moment that would change their lives forever.

If Kenna hadn't known any better she would have believed herself drunk. In a way she was, when Rory tightened his arm around her waist, awakening more than butterflies.

Leisurely, Kenna opened her eyes and met his heated gaze. "I'm sorry if I have upset ye."

A smile spread across her lips. "Ye be forgiven, dragon." She laid her head on his chest and overheard a soft growl like a primal purr escape.

Highland Destiny

They stayed in the moment, blissfully tuned, although no words flowed. Their bodies proclaimed all that needed to be said.

"Rory, can ye feel it?" Kenna asked.

"I feel a lot of things right now, lass," Rory teased.

Kenna leaned back and playfully slapped his chest. "Do no' jest."

Rory laughed. "Sorry...as ye were."

Kenna stepped out of his embrace. "Nay, the moment's gone." She crossed her arms but before she could walk away, his strong hands pulled her back into his embrace. He cupped her face and bored deep into her eyes. "I do feel it, Kenna, more than ye know. I feel ye in every fiber of me being." The truth was there swirling in those dark eyes—he meant every word.

"I feel as though my soul has known ye forever." Rory dipped his head down. Hot full lips seared her mouth when she opened herself for his kiss. His tongue was like silk as it danced with hers. This was what her mother had warned her about; the one that left you breathless, a heart-racing, toe-curling kiss. She wanted to stay like this forever, but it could never be.

Flames of desire threatened to burn out of control and Kenna had to pull away. "Rory, I..." Her breath hitched in her lungs when he sustained his hot assault down her neck. "We need to talk."

81

A rumbling vibration traveled up her skin as Rory growled in response. "Nay, nothing ye say can change me mind. I want ye, Kenna Mackenzie. I need ye now."

The throbbing need intensified immediately upon loosening the thin, leather ties that held her vest together. Strong determined fingers untied them one string at a time until Rory unbound her. Her breasts were heavy with lust and ached to be touched. She didn't have to wait long, for Rory removed her shirt in one fluid motion. Cold air hit her chest and she yearned to feel his heat.

Good sense was screaming for her to walk away, to not get involved with a dragon, and still her body defied her. Rory commanded her to surrender with an unwavering touch she craved.

"This is no' proper, Rory." A chill glided across her skin when Rory halted his sweet torture on her body. He took her head in his hands and caressed her blushing cheeks. This was it, she thought. *Ye finally pushed him away, Kenna. Is this truly what ye intended to do?*

"Lass, do ye want me?"

"Rory…'tis…complicated."

"Ye didnae answer me question. Do ye want me?" He skimmed his hand down the side of her breast and glided a thumb over her peaked nipple. "Lass, ye dinnae have to be proper wit' me."

Her need for him won over her self-control and Kenna wrapped her arms around his neck, pulling him down to claim his lips. Every part of her body begged for Rory as if she needed him like the air she breathed. Her hands shook as they roamed over his broad shoulders down to his full chest until she reached the end of his shirt. Rory broke their kiss long enough for Kenna to tug off his shirt.

"God's bones, Kenna, I could never tire of kissing ye," Rory breathed against her lips.

Kenna reached up on her toes and nipped his bottom lip. "Then dinnae stop."

~~~~~

In all his long immortal life, never had a woman awakened him the way Kenna was doing right now. It took all his resolve to hold back his dragon from claiming its mate. Kenna deserved a sweet romance, but the sting left behind on his bottom lip had driven him feral.

In one swift motion Rory grabbed Kenna's arse and picked her up as she wrapped her legs around his waist. Even through her leather trews her heat was undeniable. Rory sucked in a short breath and prayed to the Gods that he would be able to hold it together. He laid her down onto the plaid and sat back on his heels, amazed at the beauty beneath him; long, brown hair splayed out behind her head, her cheeks were flushed pink, and her lips were swollen with his kisses. Her breasts beat to the rhythm of her labored breathing, and all the while she watched his every move through lust-hooded eyes anticipating his next move.

Victoria Zak

"Kenna, ye have me word, ye are mine." Rory meant every demanding word. This was his mate and nothing would stand in his way or keep him from being with her.

Kenna reached up, grabbed him by the waist of his trews and pulled him down on top of her. "And ye are mine," she whispered into his ear while she released him from the binding material, springing his length free.

Between her hands wrapped around his cock and him trying to fumble with the laces on her pants, Rory became impatient. A sharp black claw extended from his finger and he sliced the leather from her body.

Kenna looked up at him with wide eyes. "Would ye mind warning me the next time ye do that?"

Rory smiled like the devil. "I wouldn't hurt ye if me life depended on it."

With no barriers between them their bodies ignited. Rory slinked down to the valley between her breasts, trailing hot, wet kisses as he went. Just as he fantasized, her breasts fit perfectly in his hands as he cupped them, giving them a squeeze. As he licked her peaked nipple, he looked up at her. Her head leaning back, her body arched into his, she begged for him.

Like a torturous beastie, he relentlessly continued kissing a hot trail down her stomach. Skin the color of cream craved his touch. His hands roamed every inch of her soft curves. He nipped at her pelvic bone while nudging her legs apart. He dipped his head betwixt her legs and took one long lick up the folds of her womanhood. Kenna sucked in a breath that made Rory smile devilishly.

"What are ye going to do to me, dragon?" she panted.

Rory sat back on his heels and raked his eyes down her body. The most beautiful, intoxicating lass lay before him with treasures he had sought for eons. "Hmmm, the question is what I'm no' going to do to ye. And me list is verra short." He winked.

Kenna wrapped her legs around him and pulled him on top of her. "I need ye now...dragon," she whispered seductively.

Rory's plan of sweet and slow spiraled out of control.

Though he sought to pleasure her more, the drive to be buried to the hilt overpowered all else. Inch by inch he delicately glided into Kenna's womanhood. She gripped him like a glove, pulling him deeper inside. Rory rocked his hips and pushed past her maiden's pearl, then felt like a bastard when Kenna hissed in pain.

"By the saints, Rory," she moaned.

Knowing he pleased her set him on fire and drove him farther...deeper...racing to the edge of passion to blissfully fall into the calm after the storm. Rory felt every quiver...every nail trail down his back and he relished this moment with his mate. He pleasured her in ways that left his name branded on her soul as a reminder she was all his. *Mine!*

Rory felt Kenna tightening around him. Giving her everything he had, he pumped harder until her walls crumbled away. "Rory," she whimpered.

With one last thrust Rory released. "Shite," he bit through gritted teeth as the last ripple of his climax jerked through him.

Neither moved. They stayed wrapped up in each other's arms, not wanting to let go. For Rory, his release was like nothing he had ever felt before. He now understood why his kind cherished their mates as they did. Kenna calmed him and brought out another side of him, a side he wanted to explore…the side that made him yearn for a family. And he intended on beginning to make one as soon as she was up for another round.

But there was something else. An animalistic urge of some sort commanded him to protect her at all costs, even if it meant his life. To cherish her body and soul. To pleasure her like no other. Aye, it had to be the obsessed dragon inside causing him to feel this way. The greedy bastard.

Honeysuckle drifted through the air and ignited another fire within him. He nuzzled her neck as he waited for Kenna to recover.

"Rory, is it always like this?" she asked wistfully.

Propped up on his elbows, he smoothed a lock of hair from her face. "Like what, love?"

"Like ye're floating on clouds." She teased him with feather-light caresses up and down his abdomen.

"Och, lass, I was striving for more of an engulfed in highland flames approach. Mayhap I need another chance to prove me manhood." Rory flashed his dimples at her.

"Oh, how ye make me laugh." Kenna reached up and took his head in her hands. "I've never been as complete as I am with ye, Rory Cameron."

He turned his head and kissed her palm. "As do I with you." He smiled.

Chapter Nine

"Rory, ye'll have to let me go if ye want to eat today," Kenna suggested as they held onto one another, treading the blue water of the loch. After time well spent on land, he'd picked her up, flung her over his shoulder, and made his way to the loch. They spent more time discovering each other in ways that Kenna could only describe as pure pleasure. Now, they were spent and enjoying the coolness of the loch.

Kenna started to unwrap her legs from around Rory's waist when he grabbed her hips and pulled her back into place. "I do no' want to let ye go, lass." He nuzzled her neck.

Kenna leaned her head back, allowing Rory full access. "I do no' wish to leave, but the rumbling coming from yer belly is terrifying the fish."

"Aye, lass, I have worked up a hearty appetite."

"Stay here a wee bit longer and I'll go back to the cottage and fix the evening meal." Kenna couldn't believe that they had spent all day outside. Time seemed nonexistent when she was with Rory.

"I'll let ye go for now." He winked. "But ye're mine again tonight." He kissed her then let her go.

Kenna could feel his gaze on her body as she swam to shore. Once on land she wrapped a blanket around her shoulders and darted back up the path to the cottage. She hated to leave, but indeed she too was hungry and there was one small detail to iron out. How was she going to tell Rory about her vision and how she could not marry and have children—at least not until she had another vision about her future?

Once inside, the task at hand was to find some warm clothing. Kenna dried herself off and rummaged through an auld trunk where she kept some dresses packed away. Buried beneath a few long lost treasures she pulled out a muted green dress. She'd made it out of velvet that the gypsy woman brought her. The dress—full in length with long sleeves—was perfect.

She slipped on a shift then wiggled into her dress. Turning from side to side, she viewed herself in a mirror, smoothing her hands down the soft material. The gown brought out the green in her hazel eyes, making her feel truly beautiful. Taking a brush, she combed out the tangles in her hair and hoped Rory would enjoy seeing her in something different than her leather trews. Now she was ready to fix something for them to eat.

Kenna started a fire in the hearth and brought the cauldron into the kitchen to prepare a soup. Carrots were diced, neeps were sliced, and herbs were chopped and sprinkled on top of the vegetables like snow. After

Victoria Zak

pouring some water into the cauldron to top off her soup, she returned the black pot back to the hearth so it would reach a good boil. With food preparations complete, she waited for Rory.

She gathered his pallet of blankets on the floor and was folding them when she heard Finn growling from outside. Alarmed, Kenna raced to the door and quickly went outside in search of Finn.

"Finn!" she called out. In the process of searching for the wolf, she rounded the corner of her house. Wide-eyed in shock, Kenna froze. Ears pinned back, teeth bared, and hackles up, Finn stood ready to attack...Ian?

"Ian?" Cautiously, Kenna approached as he dismounted his horse. "It can no' be."

"Kenna!" He approached her fast with excitement building up in each step. Kenna nearly stumbled as Ian drew her in, wrapping his arms around her. "I knew one day I would find ye."

Kenna stood astounded, motionless.

He released her and took a step back, holding her hands. "I've dreamt of this day since the day ye left."

The twinkle in his eyes told her that he'd never forgotten her. "Ian, how did ye find me? How did ye get past the flames?"

"Yer uncle was the one who found ye. He said he followed a gypsy woman into the glen and she led him unknowingly to ye. I thought him daft, but Kenneth was right." Ian smiled and kissed her hand.

"Ian, what about the flames?"

"I saw no flames."

Puzzled, Kenna snatched her hands away from him and ran down toward the border she had been forbidden to cross for the past five years. The flames kept her captive in the glen and kept people from reaching her. How could Ian have broken through the fire?

Dashing under low lying branches and jumping over tree stumps, Kenna finally reached the row of rowan trees and abruptly halted. Heart thumping and unable to breathe, she saw that her biggest fear had come true. The flames were gone as if they had never existed. No scorched earth, no ashes blowing into the wind, no charred grass or singed trees. "How could this be?" Crossing over uncharted territory, Kenna spun around searching for the flames. Fear slithered up her spine and her stomach cramped.

With Ian hot on her heels, it didn't take him long to catch up. "Kenna, what's going on?

Hot tears stung her eyes and threatened to fall when she turned to face him. "There were flames here, I swear on me good name."

Ian gently took her into his arms and consoled her. She didn't know whether it was out of pity or a true concern for her wellbeing, but she took in his warmth and sobbed uncontrollably. "Shhh, everything will be well again as soon as we get ye home and out of this bloody glen."

How was she supposed to protect her future son when the man she couldn't be with was here to take her back to Glenloch? There was no more hiding the truth; Kenna had to tell Ian everything. She could only hope that he would understand and accept her wishes. But she knew him well, and for him defeat would be a hard brew to swallow. Ian Mackintosh would never bow down to such a setback.

Stepping out from his embrace, Kenna shook her head and sniffed back the tears. "Ian, I can no' leave the glen, no' with ye."

Irritated with her refusal, he stood in a defensive stance with his hands on his hips. "What do ye mean ye can no' go home? Ye are promised to me."

Kenna couldn't look at him, for she could feel his frustration and hurt. "We can no' be together. This is going to sound absurd---"

"Aye, please enlighten me on this absurdity." His tone grew angrier the longer Kenna skirted around his question.

"As a wee girl growing up I had visions of events that hadn't happened yet. They were warnings of what was to come. When me parents died and me uncle sent me to stay wit' yer family, the visions stopped. I felt normal and...well, like I was living a dream that only happens to highborn lassies."

"Kenna, 'tis no' a dream. I love ye and still want ye for me wife. Ye must understand once we wed everyone will accept ye as a Mackintosh, I promise."

Kenna took another step back as he broke the space between them to cup her face. "Nay," she whispered.

Irate, Ian shoved his hand through his hair and turned his back on her. Kenna watched him pace, reeling in his anger. She thought of her next words carefully, vigilantly cautious not to snap the thin rope Ian treaded. "On the day of our wedding a vision came to me—"

"Enough!" Ian whirled around and hastily grabbed Kenna's arms. "I do no' want to hear any more nonsense!" he snarled.

"Ye have to listen to me," she begged, sobbing. "The vision was of our son. The evil I felt was dark...sinister. He had wings like a...a demon. Our son can no' be, Ian, please trust me."

The corners of his mouth fell into a grim frown, the twinkle in his eyes was replaced with enraged sorrow, and his fingers bit into her skin like a thousand needle pricks. Terror tainted her veins; she was in grave danger in his hands. She'd expected him to be angry, but never would she have believed he would hurt her, until now. "Ian! Ye're hurting me!" Fearful for her life, Kenna fought against his hold. "Let me go!"

~~~~~

Kenna! Rory's eyes popped open. Panic streamed down his spine, replacing the serenity he'd basked in most of the day, floating on his back in the loch. Interrupting the stillness of the water he lunged to his feet when a scream echoed through the glen. *Kenna!* Fighting against the water current he hiked his legs up high, hastily running to land.

Slushing through the surf, he made it to the water's edge then donned his trews that had been laid out for him on a nearby hollowed-out stump. With his heart knocking against his ribcage, every fiber in his body could feel Kenna's fear. The dragon deep within paced heavily and threatened to rear its beastie head; Rory fought to tamp down the urge to shift.

Following her honeysuckle scent, Rory trailed her footsteps back to the cottage and busted down the door without thinking twice. "Kenna!" Frantically he searched, but there was no sign of her in the small space. Intense worry set in now that he knew Kenna had to be somewhere out in the forest…alone.

Exceptional tracking abilities were Rory's finest skill. He could never be more thankful than now for that attribute as he pursued Kenna's scent through the glen. If Kenna had been hurt…he couldn't think about it, nor could he reach her fast enough.

He finally reached the row of rowan trees and his heartbeat ceased. Pure male protective instincts dove out of control as he stormed up to Ian and Kenna. He grabbed her by the waist and shoved her behind him, protecting her with his life. Face-to-face with Ian, Rory stared him down and sneered, baring his teeth, "Take yer hands off me woman." Rory shoved his fists into Ian's chest, knocking him off balance.

"Yer woman? She's betrothed to me," Ian chided.

"If ye only knew what ye're dealing wit', ye'd heed my words and walk away." Rory flashed slit pupils surrounded by dark swirls.

With nostrils flaring and teeth gritted, the men were a mere breath away. Ian grinned sinisterly. "Nay, ye have no idea who *ye're* dealing wit'." Ian flashed back a golden-yellow swirl.

Momentarily at a loss, Rory took a step back and heard Kenna gasp. "Shite." There were said to be only seven remaining Dragonkine, how could he not have known more dragons existed?

"That's right, I am a Kine and ye're breaking dragon code. Kenna is mated to me," Ian said arrogantly.

Rory looked back at Kenna. "Is this true?"

Kenna stepped out from behind Rory and slowly approached Ian, examining his eyes. "Ye're a dragon?"

"Aye."

Rory's blood boiled. That dragon had a trick up his sleeve as he watched Kenna become mesmerized by Ian's swirling eyes. "Kenna." Rory reached for her arm to pull her back to safety, but she refused and continued to be drawn deeper into Ian's gaze.

Holding her hands, Ian rubbed his thumbs gently over the inside of her wrist. "Kenna, my love, listen to me. Yer vision wasn't warning ye of me. Ye know me, I would never hurt ye. He's the stranger trying to hurt ye."

The air around them turned thick. This dragon played dirty, using magic to get what Ian wanted. Kenna fought for every breath...for her own thoughts...Shite, she was headed right into Ian's trap. Rory's dragon had nearly tolerated all he could withstand. Kenna was his and he wouldn't allow this fool to come between them.

"Nay, Ian...Rory...would no'...hurt me." Her speech was slurred.

Ian stared harder into her hazel eyes. "Ye're coming home wit' me. Ye do want to go home, dinnae ye?" Ian nodded yes like he was persuading her to decide in his favor.

"Aye, I want to go home."

"Enough!" Rory roared. "I will no' have this trickery, ye bloody bastard!" With his dragon ready on command he released the beast. Green scales rippled over his skin, spikes protruded out from his back and on the tip of his muzzle, and bones popped as they grew into an enormous dragon. A thundering roar shook the earth as razor-sharp teeth snapped at the air. His dragon soared to life.

Ian dropped Kenna's hands and pushed her out of the way. She fell hard to the ground, shaking herself free from Ian's trance. Rory growled at Ian...game on, dragon.

In a flash, Ian's human form no longer existed; a golden yellow beast replaced it. Pointed horns perched high on his head and cascaded down the sides of the beast's massive jaw. Ian stretched his wings, revealing sharp hook like talons on the top of each wing.

With all his might, Rory charged the golden beast, landing his head square into the beastie's chest, causing the dragon to stumble back. Rory snapped his teeth and bit at Ian's flesh. The fool should have known better than to come between a dragon and his mate.

Retaliating, Ian pushed back, locking horns with the green dragon. With his weight behind every push he relentlessly shoved Rory, showing him he had the upper hand and the strength to knock his cock in the dirt. In true warrior fashion, Rory fought back and ground his talons into the earth, holding his own. The dragons dueled back and forth...one step back, one step forward, they danced the battle of strength, never giving the other an inch.

The sand gave way when Rory took a step forward, causing him to slip. Seeing an advantage, Ian shouldered him, sending him off balance and off attack. Ian wasted no time and charged the green dragon, locking horns. He threw Rory to the ground by the horns, flipping him arse-over-head, then circled the fallen dragon and roared, "Ye are no' match for me. I'm more powerful and can outsmart ye. Give up now and there will be no bloodshed. I'll take Kenna home and ye can leave wit' yer life."

Wings flapped frantically as Rory strained to gain his ground back. There was no stopping him. He would fight to the death for Kenna. She was HIS MATE! With one swoop Rory brushed the ground with his wing, flinging dirt into Ian's face and nose. Ian sneezed and rapidly blinked his eyes, ridding the dirt from his vision. Like Ian, Rory saw his chance to take the dragon down. His raw male instincts urged him to kill the bastard for touching Kenna, however the Dragonkine side told him not to. The Kine needed more dragons on their side to help fight the war against Drest.

With no time to waste, Rory advanced on Ian, clamping his mouth down round Ian's throat. "Kenna is mine," he snarled through gritted teeth.

Chapter Ten

The smell of wet soil awakened her senses. Thick fog lifted to a light mist as Kenna shook off the aftereffects of Ian's magic, though her vision was hazy at best. Dirt packed underneath her nails as she dug into the glen's floor, gaining strength to pull herself up. Her arms strained to fight off the weakness settling into her bones. If she could shake the fog, perhaps she could will her body to strength.

The forest reverberated from an earth-rattling roar, causing Kenna to shudder.

Not sure she wanted to know what had made that noise, she blinked back the haze and lifted her head, brushing back the hair that stuck to her sweat-covered face. Wide-eyed, Kenna couldn't believe what she saw. "Maiden, mother, crone," she whispered.

Two immense dragons snarled and bared their teeth, salivating in bloodlust. Again she blinked until she recognized the green dragon. "Rory," she said under her breath, for her throat was too dry to talk. From the corner of her eye a shimmer stung her vision and summoned her attention. "Ian?" The gold dragon snapped at Rory, trying to pry the green dragon's mouth from its neck. Blood slithered down Ian's long neck and pooled in Rory's mouth. Deep gashes from sharp talons marred their scales and flesh. Oh merciful Heaven, they were going to kill one another if they didn't stop.

On wobbling knees Kenna stood and called out to the dragons. "Stop!" But it was of no use; they couldn't hear her through the growls and groans. In another attempt to stop this brutal dragon fight, she called out again, only to be answered by a low-bellied grunt. *Damn, stubborn beasties.*

There had to be a way to grab their attention and stop the fighting, and she wasn't going to attempt tail grabbing. Gathering up more strength, Kenna staggered unsteadily closer to the dragons. "Rory! I said stop!"

At that moment a huge green tail whipped around and slammed into her stomach, sending her crashing to the ground. Her head bounced off a rock and her world turned black.

~~~~~

"Kenna!" Rory tried to catch her fall in time, but Ian sunk his teeth into his back, breaking through scales and flesh. Rory roared, snarling in pain. Whipping around, he faced his nemesis. "Kenna's hurt!" As if the dragons were thinking on the same wavelength they shifted back to Highlanders.

"What have ye done?" Ian demanded as he ran to Kenna's side.

"I must have knocked her down in the heat of the fight." Rory reached Kenna and dropped to his knees beside her. "Kenna, can ye hear me?" Christ, she had to wake up. He hadn't heard her approach him during the fight. Rage had taken over. He hadn't meant for her to be injured.

Ian reached for Kenna to hold her and Rory growled.

"Move aside. Haven't ye done enough?" Ian bit back and began to pick Kenna up when he noticed the blood saturating her dress. "She's been stabbed." Ian glared at Rory. "Ye spiked her!"

Rory stood in disbelief as Ian proceeded to lift Kenna in his arms. Something primal within Rory stirred and drove him to protect her, heal her. "Leave her be, and that will be the last time I tell ye kindly." He shoved Ian out of the way, bent down and scooped Kenna into his arms. "Ye'll be alright, lass. I swear on me life I will make this right."

Time was of the essence and hope was fading fast. Rory released his dragon and took to the sky. Her shallow breaths pushed him farther into flight; they had to arrive at the cottage soon so he could use his healing magic to make her well.

Swooping down to the ground, without delay Rory shifted back to human and kicked down the door to the cottage. He tore through the fur wall and placed her on the bed. Extending one claw he cut through her dress to examine the extent of the puncture wound. "Shite." It was deep.

Out of nowhere Ian appeared with a pitcher of water. "'Tis no' hot, but it will do." Ian offered the pitcher to Rory.

Rory took the water and poured it over the wound then shredded a tunic that had been laid out on her bed. He washed away the pooling blood, then covered the wound with the absorbent material. Confident, Rory could stop the bleeding, his magic could heal her wound, but what he couldn't stop was the poison from his spike entering her body. Laying his hands over the cloth he closed his eyes and chanted a healing cure in his native dragon tongue.

Blood to bone

My lifeline I give to ye

Blood to bone

I heal ye

Wispy clouds of magic swirled around Kenna's body, shrouding her like a healing blanket. Rory repeated the chant over and over until the tingling magic left his body and enter hers. Opening his eyes, he lifted the bandage and the blood ceased, the gash grew together, and new pink skin held the pieces together. Rory briefly exhaled. Alas, Kenna's life was still at stake. Deadly poison flowed through her veins. Although it took large doses of his venom to affect or even kill a dragon, for a human, one prick could cause death.

Rory removed the rest of her clothes. God's teeth, she had looked beautiful in that dress.

"How is she?"

Ian looked over Rory's shoulder at his naked mate. "Bloody hell, man, show some respect." Rory covered her body with a plaid.

Swiftly Ian turned his back and crossed his arms over his chest. "I'm concerned."

"Well, she is of no concern to ye. Leave."

"I will no'. Not until Kenna tells me to leave, and the way I see it...she'll be rid of ye before she tells me to leave."

Rory busied himself, tucking blankets around her, because if his hands were free he would have hauled off and punched the cocky bastard.

On bent knees, Rory took her hand in his. So delicate. He kissed her palm and rubbed her forearm then he abruptly paused. Dark purple veins sprang from paling skin and pumped the poison through her body. Rory hung his head and cursed himself for a fool a thousand times over. Only time would tell if his feisty brunette would have enough strength to fight off the venom. There was nothing more he could do.

Night had fallen fast, covering the sky in darkness. Hours had been long and daunting as Rory tended to Kenna's every need. During the night Kenna broke with fever and chills that shook her body uncontrollably. For a while death lingered over her, as Rory couldn't bring her fever down. He dabbed her forehead and neck countless times with cool, wet cloths while he prayed to the Gods that they would allow him to take her place. Hopelessness sank in as he watched the poison take over more and more of her body.

Sometime during the early morn Rory awoke to Kenna restlessly moving her head back and forth, fighting back the pain. Rory rushed to her side to find the fever had broken, and she weakly opened her eyes. "Kenna, ye've come back to me." Every prayer he made had been answered.

A frail smile spread across her lips, but that smile wasn't for him. Rory followed her eyes over his shoulder and saw Ian standing behind him. He didn't want to cause another disturbance, so he excused himself from her bedside before he did something stupid like punch that ardent grin from Ian's face. It was perfectly clear she'd chosen between the two dragons. Hell, he didn't blame her for choosing Ian. In the heat of battle Rory had lost his head, which cost him his true love.

"What a fool," he spat as he poured himself a tankard of ale, bringing the rest of the pitcher with him to the table. He sat down heavily and drained the tankard. Over and over again the image of Kenna falling to the ground ran through his mind like a never-ending nightmare. Now he had the time to process every gut gnawing detail of the night's events and the odds were stacked against him. He sure as hell wouldn't forgive himself. He was a helpless, out of control fool in love with Kenna and had made his first and last mistake. "A dragon in love," he mumbled under his breath, pouring another round of ale.

Rory's leg thumped a rhythmic beat on the floor as he fought the urge to throw Ian out on his arse. Everything about the cocky bastard irritated him to the marrow. He watched the fool brush back her hair, lean over and kiss her forehead. Bile rose in the back of his throat with the thought of Ian confessing his undying love for her. Christ, he wished he could hear what the Kine was saying to her.

It should be him over there with Kenna, not Ian. Draining the tankard dry, he slammed the damn thing on the table. If this was what love felt like, a sword to the gut, then damn the Gods for trusting him with a mate. Rory peered over at Ian and held back a snarl. He didn't know who he was most angry at: Ian or himself for acting a fool.

Ian left Kenna's bedside and joined him, pouring himself a tankard of ale, and sat down across from the brooding Highlander. "She's sleeping now." Ian drank from the tankard then placed it on the table. "Once she's well rested I'll be taking her back home wit' me."

Appalled at Ian's shrewdness, Rory bit back the urge to lash out. He cleared his throat. "Is this what Kenna wants?"

"It does no' matter what she wants, 'tis what's best for her." Ian confidently leaned back in his chair.

"What do ye mean she has no choice? She's a grown woman capable of making her own decisions. Ye can no' make her leave if she does no' want to."

Ian chuckled at Rory. "Ye need to understand something, Kenna is me wife to be. I didnae search high and low for her for five years for nothing. Regardless of her visions, we'll be wed."

"Visions?"

"She didn't tell ye?"

"Nay." Rory's dark brows furrowed.

"Kenna can no' have children with a Dragonkine. I've known this all along, but frankly I do no' care. As long as she is mine." Ian drained the tankard then wiped his mouth with the back of his hand. He glared at Rory, daring him to disagree.

"Ye be mistaken. She can no' have children wit' ye because I'm her mate and furthermore…" Rory stood, knocking the chair over behind him. He slammed his hands on the table and leaned across, coming face to face with Ian. "Ye'll have to kill me before I allow her to leave here with ye."

Ian stood slowly and challenged Rory. "We'll see aboot that when she wakes, now won't we?" Ian's smirk struck Rory in the gut as if he had punched him. What had the bastard done?

Alpha virile strength between the two dragons permeated the room, fueling the tension to shift and destroy one another. Rory couldn't fight it. His dragon was relentless, pacing back and forth, chomping at the bit to be released. At the end of his tether, large claws scraped deep trails across the tabletop as Rory gripped the wood and flipped the table over onto Ian. "What did ye say to her, ye bloody bastard?" Rory seethed.

Chapter Eleven

The room came into view slowly when Kenna opened her eyes and saw Rory next to her on the bed. Or had she been dreaming? A sense of ease replaced the shivers that had made her body quake. For how long she'd fought the fever she did not know. All that mattered was that the blistering, searing pain flowing through her veins had vanished.

As she struggled to recall what had caused her pain, she looked up and saw Ian standing over Rory's shoulder. His gaze heated her body and she felt like her head was in the clouds. *Wait, why is Rory leaving?*

Words had come out of Ian's mouth in a jumbled stream of confusion. Kenna struggled hard to understand him, but she was losing the ability to recover, slipping in and out of consciousness. She heard Ian telling her that he wanted her to come home, that he loved her, and they would overcome the obstacles that stood in their way. They could be happy again.

Her eyes fluttered open when she heard Rory's name. As quickly as her heart skipped a beat and she felt her soul settle, it suddenly plummeted to the ground.

"Kenna, ye can no' trust Rory. He's unstable, he poisoned ye."

Poison? Rory? She mouthed the words in disbelief. She sat up and the room spun. Ian ordered her to lay back down and rest.

Fighting the urge to slip back into sleep, Kenna shook her head forcefully, battling back the haze. It was of no use; the fog thickened, her body surrendered, and she drifted out of consciousness again.

Voices paraded around in her head like mist as her restless mind came to. The tension in the air was as thick as the infuriated tone in the voices she heard from across the room. A crash startled Kenna and she sat up quickly. Mayhap a little too quickly. A shot of pain like lightning struck her head.

Kenna huffed and swung her legs over the side of the bed. Once she gained enough strength, she crossed the room and stood with her arms crossed over her chest by the hearth. Glaring at the men, she remained there watching them. The table was turned upside down, ale pooled on the floor from a pitcher, and Rory had Ian backed up against the wall with his hands wrapped around her betrothed's neck. They were too busy quarreling over her to realize she was even awake. This had to stop.

Finn, who had been lying at her bedside, stood and went to Kenna. He sat down by her feet, watching the dueling dragons. "Finn, this has to stop now," Kenna said.

Finn looked up at her and blinked as if he agreed.

"This has gotten out of control," she said out loud, hoping the Highlanders would hear her warning. She tapped her fingers on her arm. "I believe our guests have overstayed their welcome."

Snarling, Finn stood and snapped at the air towards the fools.

"Kenna." Rory loosened his grip and hurried over to her. "Ye're awake."

Before Rory could reach her, Finn took a step forward and growled, warning him to back away.

"Aye, and ye would have known sooner if ye weren't fighting wit' Ian."

Coughing overdramatically, Ian played the victim. "Kenna...'tis good to see ye well." He rubbed his throat and glared crossly at Rory.

"For God's sake Ian, ye're no' hurt," Kenna huffed. "I want ye oot of me house, now."

"Kenna—" Ian's eyes began to swirl as he stared at her.

"Dinnae use yer magic on me. Ye betrayed me trust. Why didnea ye tell me ye were a dragon?"

"I...I—"

"It does no' matter. I want ye to leave. Now, Ian." Kenna pointed her chin to the door.

"Yer making a huge mistake, Kenna," he pleaded.

"'Tis already a mistake. I should never have accepted yer marriage proposal."

"Aye, and ye dinnae take another dragon's mate." Rory said with a half-cocked smile of victory.

Ian bit back, "Nor do ye poison her."

Kenna turned her sights on Rory. No emotion shone through her stone cold features. She swallowed hard and straightened her spine. Because of his overbearing jealousy, she could have lost her life. "I want ye to leave as well, Rory."

"Kenna, ye can no mean it."

Rory approached Kenna and reached out to brush her cheek, but she turned away from his touch. "Kenna, look at me." Strong hands cupped her face and before she knew what was happening, she was staring into his dark smoldering eyes. The soft kindness in his face that she adored had turned hard. Being this close, the heat between them threatened to burn all her resolve to ashes.

Rory dipped his head until she could feel his breath across her lips. "Ye know me, Kenna. I never meant to hurt ye. Aye, I was foolish and I be sorry for it for the rest of me life. Please, I'm asking for yer forgiveness."

Kenna closed her eyes tightly, trying to fight back the tears that threatened to streak down her cheeks. Her body shook, threatening to crumble into a million sorrowful pieces. Lumps formed in her throat, making it difficult for her to speak.

She opened her eyes and pulled away from Rory and shook her head no. "I can no'..." She couldn't finish her thought before the tears rolled uncontrollably from her eyes. Her heart shattered when she saw the hurt on his face.

Rory took her hands in his. "Ye know us." He placed her hands on his heart. "I love ye, lass."

Stoic, Kenna held his gaze. "If ye love me, then let me go. Forget ye ever knew me. I will only bring ye sorrow."

"Kenna—"

"Leave. Now."

Rory turned and strode toward the door, stopping to turn the table back on its legs. Kenna flinched as the door slammed shut behind both men. She fell to her knees, sobbing into Finn's fur. There was no other choice to be made. She had forbidden herself to be with either one. Protecting her unborn son was top priority and she would hold to the promise she'd made to herself years ago. Her son's life depended on her good judgment, not happiness.

Chapter Twelve

Days morphed into weeks and soon a long numbing month had passed Kenna by. After there were no more tears to be shed and she could no longer stand lying in bed anymore, Kenna became emotionless as she tried to live a life without Rory, which was impossible, since everything in the cottage reminded her of him. There was now an empty hole inside her that nothing filled. Tinkering with her latest weapon invention used to absorb her and make her feel strong, but not anymore. Today she worked with a distracted mind.

Kenna sat at the wooden table sharpening a blade that had gone dull from lack of use. With other things on her mind, the stone slipped from her fingers and she sliced her hand on the blade. "Bloody hell!" She strode to the washbasin and rinsed the blood from her hand. The cut was deep. Wrapping a cloth around it, Kenna sighed and looked out the window in front of her. The flames were back and higher than before. They blazed furiously to the sky and threatened to singe the billowing clouds.

Time and again she asked herself if she had made the right decision in letting both men go. If she followed her heart, the answer was no. Kenna hung her head and tapped the wall with her booted foot. After searching for her for five long years, Ian deserved to find happiness with a worthy woman, for she could never return his love. Aye, there had been a time when she thought she could fit into his world and he was the right one for her, but that had been a lie.

Then Rory had entered her life, scorched her soul and made her feel again, showing her how to live in the moment. But in doing so she had been reckless and put the future of her son in jeopardy. Kenna took in a deep breath. She'd made the right decision. Her memory of Rory would fade over time. Would it not?

Kenna examined her hand. The throbbing lessened to a mere sting. Ever since she had been poisoned by Rory's spike, she healed more quickly than usual. She shrugged her shoulders. "Must be the magic of the dragon," she whispered as she sat back down at the table, examining her wound, when a knock at the door startled her.

Finn was already at the door when Kenna opened it. She was pleasantly surprised to see the auld gypsy woman cloaked in black, waiting to be invited in. "Good day, Kenna."

"Good day, please come in. Sit. I… " Kenna looked over at the kitchen and frowned. With her mind muddled with the past, she hadn't hunted, picked berries, nor cleaned in weeks.

"Do no' fash yerself, child." The woman waved off Kenna's concern. "I have brought goodies of me own to share." The auld gypsy sat a basket down on the table and took out fresh bread, cheese, and wine. "I be terribly sorry for no' coming sooner, but I've been a wee bit busy. I hope ye have fared well?" She lowered her hood and took off her cloak.

With a huff Kenna sat down across from the woman. Time had been good to the gypsy. Her hair was still streaked gray, which matched the color in her eyes. And the corners of her mouth still wrinkled when she smiled. Oh how she had missed that smile. There was a comfort, a sense of wisdom about the woman that Kenna couldn't explain.

"Child, what be on yer mind?" The woman peered across the table at her.

"I dinnae know where to start. I'm so confused." Kenna looked down into her lap at Finn who was resting his head on her legs. "'Tis silly. Ye'll think I'm daft and I'm sure ye dinnae have the time to listen to me woes."

"Och, my sweetling, I have nothing but time." The woman smiled.

Her voice was so lovely, so calming that Kenna could confide in the gypsy as if she was her own mother. "Do ye believe in dragons?" Kenna traced the claw trails that marred her table. Another reminder of Rory.

"Aye, I do. They carry a mighty magic." The graying woman busied herself handing out the provisions in her basket.

"I met one…actually two. They happen to be human as well."

The woman paused and sat down, giving Kenna her full attention. "Go on."

"His name is Rory. At first I thought the dragon was the one setting the flames, but he wasn't. He was kind to me even after I shot him with Dragon Slayer."

"Dragon Slayer? Ye shot him?"

"Aye, but I didnae hurt him. He claims to love me."

"I must say if he still claims to love ye after ye threatened his life, he's worth keeping, aye?"

Kenna shook her head. "I wish it was that easy. Things turned ugly once Ian showed up."

"Eejit." The woman spat under her breath.

Kenna looked at the gypsy with suspicious eyes. "Do ye know Ian Mackintosh?"

The woman quickly sliced the bread. "Aye. He's the second dragon ye speak of? The name does sound familiar."

"Aye, I was going to be his bride."

"I know, child."

Kenna froze at the woman's confession. "What do ye mean? Do ye know why I'm here?"

The woman exhaled deeply and held Kenna's hands. "I was there at the market that day, warning ye to seek oot the glen. I knew the time would come when ye would see a vision of yer future son and ye would need to run far away from Ian."

That explained why she felt she had seen the woman before. Back at the market Kenna hadn't gotten a good look at the gypsy. "So, me visions are true. If I marry, my son will become an evil tyrant."

An intensity radiated from the auld woman "'Tis crucial ye listen to yer visions, Kenna."

"But why? Why do I have these visions? I feel as though I've lived my revelations when they come to me."

"That's because yer soul has, child. Yer soul jumps through time. That's how ye have invented all these futuristic weapons. 'Tis how ye know that Ian is no' yer true love."

Kenna looked at the woman as if she had grown two heads. Everything she said sounded absurd, however it explained what she had been going through most of her life.

"What aboot the flames?"

"I've cast these highland flames around ye for a reason, child. To lure yer true love to ye and shield you from those who would interfere."

"How can that be when I can no' marry and have wee ones of me own?"

"No one said that ye can no' have wee ones. Ye need yer true love and Ian is no' it. That's why yer vision warned ye."

"Ye set these highland flames around me to keep me here until my true love finds me?"

"Aye, I needed to protect ye, my sweetling. An auld crone like me may no' have the brawn, but I can outsmart a dragon like Ian Mackintosh." The woman paused, allowing Kenna to absorb this newfound information. "There are things ye might no' understand right now. But in time ye'll see why yer visions are so important. Ye must follow them."

Taken aback, Kenna sank into the chair. "I dinnae understand. If the flames were conjured to keep Ian from finding me, why did he find me anyway?"

The crone exhaled deeply. "Because the flames were set to bring yer true love to ye. Once he found ye the spell was lifted and the flames burned oot."

Kenna couldn't believe what she was hearing, but it made sense. *The flames are what brought me here to ye,* she recalled Rory telling her. Wait…Rory was her true love?

Kenna sobbed in her hands. *What have I done?*

"Me sweetling, what be the matter?"

"I've ruined everything," she sobbed through breaths of air. "I sent me true love away."

118

"Bah!" The woman protested. "One can never send true love away. Ye have to find him and bring him back home."

Kenna wiped the tears from her eyes and sniffed back the sorrow. A gleam of hope rose inside her. "Aye, I must find him, but how?"

"Follow the flames." The auld woman pointed to the window. Following the woman's wrinkled finger, Kenna saw the highland flames appear higher and brighter than before. Kenna beamed and looked back at the woman. "Go on now, child, yer love awaits."

Excitement billowed over Kenna as she raced to grab her cloak. "Come, Finn." She reached the door and opened it, but before she crossed the threshold she turned to face the woman. "Oot of all the times we met, I never asked yer name."

"Me name is Gertrude."

"Thank ye, Gertrude."

"It be me pleasure, lass. Sometimes it takes a nest of flames to protect the ones ye love. Now go, yer dragon awaits."

With one last smile at Gertrude, Kenna ran out the door and to the flames.

Chapter Thirteen

The flames licked at the sky in shades of orange and yellow as the sun tucked behind the clouds. She'd been following a single row of blaze all day and there seemed to be no end. Kenna picked up the pace, for she didn't want to be out in the glen when night fell. The flames burned on and on.

Hot on Rory's trail, she prayed he would forgive her for acting too hastily. All along she supposed there was a part of her that knew she was meant to be with him; she only wished she had seen it sooner. No one had ever made her feel thoroughly loved like Rory had. With one touch, one smile, or one smoldering glare he'd showed her how much she meant to him.

The flames turned to the east then leveled out straight. When Kenna turned the corner she slowed down to take a breath. "Finn, I do wish I knew where we are headed." She turned around, searching the area for some kind of protection. Night was upon them and she needed to seek shelter. Wild boar roamed these parts of the Highlands, and with no weapons, she would prefer not to come in contact with the beasts.

With his nose to the wind, Finn stood at attention as if he smelled a familiar scent. "What is it?" Trepidation pricked her skin in fear of the unknown. Slowly Finn stalked along the row of flames and Kenna followed closely behind, trusting that the wolf knew what he was doing.

Before long they came to a wall of flames allowing no passage. Kenna stood with her hands on her hips, searching for a way around. "I dinnae understand. We've hit a dead end and there's no sign of Rory anywhere."

Flames roared in front of her, mocking, taunting her emotions as if they were laughing at her. How was she going to get through this blazing wall without catching on fire? What if Rory was right on the other side? "Rory!"

The blaze crackled in response.

Kenna's heart sank into the pit of her stomach. How could she have been such a naïve fool in trusting the auld crone? She had been deceived. Again. Fury welled into rage as she picked up a rock and threw the blasted thing into the incendiary abyss.

She plopped down in front of a tree and slumped over from pure exhaustion. Defeated, hungry, and heartbroken, she wondered why life was being so cruel. Hours passed as Kenna sat; she sobbed, she raged, she mourned until there was no hope left. Again she had set herself up to be fooled. Never again.

A cold wind blew, chilling her and telling her it was time to go home.

Kenna rubbed the chill from her arms and stood peering into the flames. Nothing had changed. They still danced and licked sky high. Sighing, she prepared to walk back to her cottage. "Come, Finn." Looking over her shoulder to see if the gray wolf followed, Kenna gasped. Turning around, she was astounded by what she saw; the flames parted like a curtain being pulled back. Kenna stepped closer. An opening came into view as more of the blaze disappeared, revealing a black shimmering cave. "Maiden, mother, crone," she gasped.

Finn knocked his massive body against her thigh as he raced past her and into the dark cave. "Finn!" Kenna yelled after him, but he didn't stop. Reaching the mouth of the cave, she peeked in and saw nothing but darkness. "Finn!"

Kenna grabbed a nearby branch and held it to the flames, igniting it, then entered the cave. Once she was inside, the torch cast eerie shadows on the rock walls as she crept down the stone-walled chamber, careful not to trip over the rocky path. A noise from behind made her jump and swing her torch in front of her. "Bloody hell!" A rat scurried and disappeared into the darkness. Even the smallest of noises sounded menacing in the echoing blackness. Taking a deep breath, Kenna bit back the fear and continued downward.

Stalactites hung from the ceiling and stretched to the ground, creating thick pillars. Drips of water from smaller stalactites pooled into puddles, and the drip, drip of water echoed throughout the cavern. The smell of wet earth lingered and chilled the air.

After Kenna made her way down a long corridor, the cave widened into a massive open space. Lit torches lined the foremost wall and black stones embedded in the rock walls shimmered and twinkled under Kenna's torch. She reached out and ran her finger over the shiny object in awe of its beauty, looking down abruptly when she felt the ground change from hard to soft. Furs from wall to wall covered the ground. She bent down and stroked the softness when she heard a vibrating grunt echo through the cave.

Movement that sounded like something was being dragged against the floor startled her. She wasn't alone. Blackness covered the back wall of the cave. There had to be a creature lurking in the shadows. Kenna swallowed hard and pressed on.

Finding the courage to move forward—or perhaps it was curiosity gnawing at her—Kenna crept toward the shadow. A long green tail with sharp spikes slowly slithered into the light. "Rory?" Kenna shined her torch into the darkness, causing the green dragon to look at her. "Rory."

Her smile quickly changed to a frown when he turned his head and blew out the torch. He growled, swishing his tail ever so slightly—and threateningly.

Kenna did not flinch. It was quite apparent he didn't want her here, but bloody hell, she hadn't followed the flames for nothing. At best, he would have to hear what she had to say. At that moment, she realized in her soul what she should have known all along. "Ye said ye could never hurt me. I know it's true, Rory. I know it here." She pressed her fist to her heart.

Quirking his devilish dragon brows, he stared at her skeptically, in silence.

"I should have trusted ye," Kenna continued, though the dragon did not appear the least bit interested. "I do trust ye—"

Rory hissed in disbelief.

Gathering all her courage about her, Kenna swallowed painfully and went on, though her heart was breaking. "But my head was muddled that day. I'd no' quite recovered from the fever." Another hiss interrupted her. She tried to meet his eyes, but he would not come out of the darkness.

"I came all this way to tell ye—I just wanted ye to know how much I love ye. I always will." It was as if the words were wrenched from her. There. She'd said it

Rory's dragon stretched out, still silent, filling most of the space, leaving Kenna little room to walk around him. Scooting along the wall, she smoothed her hands down his neck, letting him know her touch. Heedful, she bent down on her knees and lifted his head into her hands. "Rory, ye must listen. It was wrong of me to send ye away. I know better now. Because of the vision I had five years ago, I always thought I was to be alone. It was the only way I could protect my future son. But now I know, 'tis ye I belong to. Ye are me true love, Rory."

Kenna laid her forehead against the ridge of his nose. She felt his warm breath against her skin as he exhaled. The dragon lifted his head from her hands and backed away from her, glowering. She felt empty and chilled beyond measure.

"Rory? Where are ye going?" Kenna watched as he moved away to another part of the cave.

Weak, she stood tall and placed her hands on her hips. "Please say something."

The dragon disappeared.

Bewildered, Kenna stood in the middle of the room wondering why he had not even acknowledged her presence. In the short time she had associated with dragons one thing was certain; dragons were stubborn.

A deeper silence filled the room, leaving Kenna defeated in her attempt to bring her dragon back home. "I see I've wasted me time." She pushed back the tears and hid them behind the wall she'd put up, protecting herself from further heartache. She straightened her spine and took a deep breath. "I'll leave ye be, but know this…there will never be another I love more than ye, dragon."

Kenna lifted a torch off the wall. She glanced through the hollow, echoing cave one last time, then made her way back down the dark corridor.

Tears breached the wall she had tried so hard to hold up. Each determined stride she took toward the exit brought more tears down her cheeks. Through sobbing breaths she gasped for air, but the air that lingered over the corridor was too thick. Kenna squinted ahead and was relieved to see the night's twinkling stars ahead. A few steps farther and she would be out of the cave.

As she reached the opening, strong arms wrapped around her waist and pulled her back into the darkness.

"Lass, if ye think I'm going to let ye walk oot of this cave, ye must be daft." Rory's breath against her skin sent chills down her spine. She leaned her head to the side while he assaulted her neck with hot searing kisses. "Christ, Kenna, I've missed ye."

"I'm so sorry… I…"

"Shhh. I should be the one asking ye for forgiveness. I acted a fool." She felt Rory pulling and tugging at the leather straps of her vest until he ripped the material off her body. God's teeth, she couldn't think straight. Rory's hands slipped under her tunic and cupped her breasts.

"I should probably welcome ye properly into me lair," he murmured against her ear.

"Hmmm. 'Tis dark outside and the Highlands are no place for a lass come nightfall." Kenna reached behind her and rubbed Rory's thighs.

"Aye, it wouldn't be verra gentlemanlike to send a wee lass out in the dark to fend for herself."

126

Rory hissed as her hands traveled gingerly closer to his length with teasing caresses. "I think it be wise for me to stay at least until the morn," Kenna declared breathlessly as she swayed her arse against the stiffness of his shaft.

With one fluid motion, Rory spun her around and captured her lips, kissing her with a passion she felt soul deep, a connection undeniable. She was whole again.

Rory broke their bond for a brief moment. He brushed his hands into her long, brown hair and gazed upon her as if he was truly seeing her for the first time. "Kenna Mackenzie, be me wife."

Speechless, Kenna beheld his smoldering dark eyes that possessed an intensity she could feel in her bones. Rory Cameron was asking her to be his wife, to have wee ones, to be his forever.

"Lass, I promise to be a good husband."

Kenna giggled, wiping away a stray tear. "Aye, I will be yer wife." She threw her arms around his neck and kissed him.

"Och, ye had me worried for a while. I thought perhaps ye had grown tired of dragons," he jested.

"Nay." Kenna took his head in her hands, thumbing over his full lips. "Ye're me dragon for always."

Rory whispered against her lips as he picked her up into his arms and carried her back into his dragon's lair, "Always."

About the Author

Victoria Zak is an international best-selling author of the Scottish Historical Paranormal Romance series the Guardians of Scotland. Her first book Highland Burn, was a 2015 RONE award finalist for best paranormal romance. She has also written in the World of DeWolfe Pack, Amazon Kindle Worlds, for USA Today best-selling author Kathryn Le Veque.

When not conjuring her next story, Victoria enjoys spending time with her husband and two kids.

Victoria loves to hear from her readers. You can connect with her through the links below:

Website www.victoriazakromance.com

@VictoriaZak2

https://www.facebook.com/VictoriaZakAuthor

Books by Victoria Zak

Guardians of Scotland Series:

Highland Burn

Highland Storm

Highland Fate

Highland Destiny

Hell's Cowboys Series

My Immortal Cowboy

Kiss Me Deadly (2017)

Hell on My Heels (2017)

Stand Alones

Once Upon a Winter Solstice

De Wolfe's Honor

The Jewel of Grim Fortress

CPSIA information can be obtained
at www.ICGtesting.com
Printed in the USA
LVOW07s2156020117
519496LV00003B/258/P